Tilly's Moonlight Garden

Julia Green

sourcebooks
jabberwocky

Published by Sourcebooks Jabberwocky, an imprint of Sourcebooks, Inc.
P.O. Box 4410, Naperville, Illinois 60567-4410
(630) 961-3900
Fax: (630) 961-2168
www.jabberwockykids.com

Originally published in Great Britain in 2012 by Oxford University Press.

Library of Congress Cataloging-in-Publication data is on file with the publisher.

Source of Production: Bang Printing, Brainerd, Minnesota, USA
Date of Production: September 2012
Run Number: 18379

Printed and bound in the United States of America.
BG 10 9 8 7 6 5 4 3 2 1

For my parents,
Barbara and Reg Green
with love

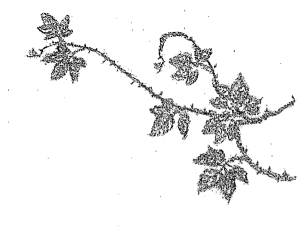

All day, the fox tried to sleep, curled up with the tip of its tail wrapped around its body, but its ears twitched, listening for danger.

As evening came and shadows lengthened across the grass, the truck drove away. The front door banged shut. At last it was quiet—just the normal sounds of an autumn evening. A blackbird sang at the top of a tree. A squirrel ran along the edge of the rickety wooden fence.

The fox uncurled itself. It yawned and stretched.

Silently, on velvet paws, it slipped through the bars of the gate into the garden. No one saw its slim, red-brown body and long tail as it stopped at the edge of the lawn to sniff the night air. It looked up at the house.

The fox called out into the dark. It was a strange sound, an eerie, high-pitched scream that echoed around the night garden and made everything afraid.

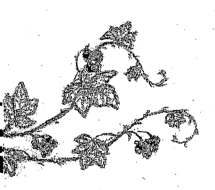

Chapter 2

Tilly's spine tingled. She uncurled her legs from under the blanket, slid off the sofa, and went to the window to look out. What had made that horrible noise? But it was dark outside; all she could see was her own reflection in the glass, staring back at her.

"Tilly?" Dad called from upstairs. "Time to get ready for bed. I'll come and say good night later."

Tilly opened the living room door. The hall was dark. A tiny bit of yellowy light shone in from the streetlight outside, through the pane of glass above the front door, just enough to fill the hall with shadowy creatures. The stairs seemed to lead up into a yawning, black nothing.

Tilly waited, in case that scary screaming sound came again. It was so quiet in the house she could hear the tick, tick, tick of the clock on the kitchen wall. She took a deep breath. She made herself step into the shadowy dark. She dashed to the bottom of the stairs, reached up to the light switch, and flicked it on.

There! Now she could see it was just the hallway, with coats hanging on pegs, cold tiles on the floor, and a staircase with a strip of green carpet going up the middle, held tight by gold metal rods on each step.

Everything in this house was old-fashioned and strange and smelled funny. The ceilings were high up and there were plaster flowers in the middle where the lights hung from. It was much bigger than their old house. It was almost big enough, Tilly thought, to get lost in. The furniture was big and dark too—wardrobes and cupboards and tables and chairs and pictures in heavy gold frames that had belonged to the old lady who had lived in the house before she died. The walls had old-fashioned wallpaper, with patterns of flowers and birds.

They would change all that, Dad said. Paint the whole house, top to bottom, to freshen it up. Get rid of some of the furniture that the old lady had left behind and make the house more theirs. Eventually.

It would be a good house for playing hide-and-seek in, Tilly thought. But she didn't know anyone around here to play with. Not yet. In her old neighborhood, where the houses were all joined together and went in steps down the hill, all the children dashed in and out of each other's houses every day after school and all day on the weekend. Her best friend, Ally, lived in the house two doors down. And now they were all miles and miles away.

Tilly went up the bit of stairs that turned the corner, and then along the hallway. The carpet was soft, like moss under her feet. It went in a strip, with bare brown boards on either side. She was careful to stay in the middle. The dark wood on either side was shiny, like water. She was on a moss bridge, going over a river, and if she fell…

Tilly stopped outside Mom's bedroom door. She listened. Not a sound. There was no strip of light shining out from under the door. Mom must be asleep. For a moment, Tilly thought about pushing open the heavy door, tiptoeing in to kiss Mom good night…

But she mustn't wake Mom up. Mom wasn't very well. Just as they'd unpacked the very last boxes, Mom's head started hurting so much she had to go and lie down.

And then it got much worse, and the doctor came, and all Tilly's excitement about moving to the new house got swallowed up in worrying about Mom.

The doctor said Mom needed to sleep so she could get better faster, and so that the baby would be all right. The baby was growing inside Mom; it needed to grow a lot more before it was ready to be born in early spring.

"So, please be extra quiet and helpful, Tilly," Dad said when the doctor had gone, "because I've got enough on my plate already."

Tilly padded on past the shut door, along to her own room. She stretched her hand up through the open gap and switched on the light. What was that scuttling under the bed? She shivered again.

She knew what Dad would say. "Old houses are full of noises. It's the radiator clunking and gurgling, water running along old pipes. It's only the draft from the window making the curtain twitch. You've such a vivid imagination, Tilly!"

Tilly turned on the night-light next to the bed. She picked up her neatly folded pajamas from her pillow and took them with her to the bathroom next door. It was a small room, so you could see into all its corners right away, and it was bright with white tiles and shiny faucets and the towels hanging on a warm rod. Tilly washed her hands and face, and brushed her teeth. She put on her pink rose-patterned pajamas and slippers. She padded back to the bedroom and closed the door and turned off the big light and climbed into bed to wait for Dad to finish his work and come upstairs to say good night.

The night-light on the bedside table glowed like a moon. Little Fox was waiting for her, tucked under the blanket where no one else could see him. She knew she was too old, really, for night-lights and stuffed animals. But Little Fox was different. Tilly stroked his furry red-brown head against her cheek. His nose and eyes were shiny bright, and his ears and paws had black tips, but the tip of his tail and his chest were white. Little Fox had been with Tilly forever and ever. She had stroked and loved him so much he had a bald patch on the back of his head.

She waited for ages, but still Dad didn't come.

The fox called again. Its eerie cry echoed into the night.

The sound wove in and out of the night garden and into Tilly's dreams.

Chapter 3

In the silvery light of dawn, everything looked different. The shadows in the room were dove gray. The cupboard with the framed photo on it of the last house, her bathrobe hanging on the back of the door, her old toy box, and the shelves of books were all soft gray shapes, as if they were waiting for proper daylight for the real colors to come back in.

Tilly listened.

Why had she woken up? Had there been a noise?

Sometimes she woke up in the middle of the night and she thought she could still hear the echo of something, some sound. But she couldn't say what, exactly, she had heard.

The house breathed deeply, as if it was sleeping.

Mom was sleeping. Dad was sleeping.

Tilly climbed out of bed. She padded across the carpet to the curtains and pulled them back just enough to make a gap, so she could see out of the window.

A fox trotted across the lawn below. Its black feet left silver prints in the damp grass. It stopped, looked up at Tilly at the window. For a moment it stood still as a statue, one paw lifted up, ears pricked up, and watched her. It looked deep into her eyes.

Tilly pressed her face closer to the cold window glass. The fox turned, trotted on across the grass, and disappeared between two silvery-gray bushes.

Tilly's breath misted the glass; she rubbed it clear again but there was no sign of the fox now, just its faint prints left behind in the damp grass. The garden lay still and waiting, full of gray shadows. Tilly shivered. She climbed down off the windowsill and crept back into bed, under the warm blanket. Her hand reached out for Little Fox, but he must have fallen out of the bed, and before Tilly could climb out again to find him, she was drifting back into sleep.

Tilly thought about the real fox while she was at school the next day. When Dad came for her after school, she nearly told him what she had seen. But she didn't. She kept the fox her secret.

"How's Mom?" Tilly asked him as they went into the house.

"Resting. But you can see her later and tell her about your day. Now, I've got work to do. Why don't you play in the garden till teatime, Tilly?"

Tilly sat for a while on the seat under the big tree in the middle of the lawn. The garden was warm in the afternoon sunshine. Even though it was late autumn, bees buzzed from one pink flower to another in the flower bed next to the hedge. Flies that looked like tiny wasps, but weren't, hovered over yellow flowers next to a wigwam of sticks holding up withered, old bean plants. White butterflies flitted over the cabbage patch. The old lady who used to live here had loved her vegetable garden. "When we get ourselves organized," Dad had said, "we'll grow our own vegetables too."

Not cabbages, Tilly hoped. She got up and walked across the grass, the same way the fox had gone so early this morning. The sun had dried the grass; no paw prints were left. She found the two silvery bushes and went between them, brushing against the leaves that looked more green than silver now and left a strong smell on her hands. On the other side there was a metal gate.

Tilly peered through. A grassy path went in both directions, left and right, and just across the other side was another gate, but wooden and tumbledown. Where did that go?

"Tilly? Tilly?" Dad called.

Tilly ran back to the lawn.

Dad put a tray down on the grass next to the seat under the tree. There was a blue mug of tea for him and Tilly's pink mug for her. Dad had made sandwiches.

"Peanut butter," he said. "And banana."

Tilly wrinkled up her nose. Dad had a funny idea about what tasted nice in sandwiches.

"Have one," Dad said. "It's a long time until supper."

Tilly wasn't hungry. She hadn't been hungry since Mom got ill.

She nibbled the corner of a sandwich. The peanut butter made her tongue sticky and thick and horrible.

A small bird flew down from the tree and landed on the grass. It looked at Tilly with its beady eye, its head to one side. Tilly picked off a crumb of sandwich and threw it. The bird hopped forward and picked up the crumb. It flew back up to the branch, above Tilly's head.

Crumb by crumb, the bird ate all of Tilly's sandwich. Dad didn't notice. He was busy drinking his tea and thinking. Absentmindedly, Dad ate the other three sandwiches. Tilly knew he was in the middle of writing something, and all he was thinking about was the next bit of his story. That was the trouble with having a dad who was a writer. Most of the time, she didn't mind.

Dad slurped up the last sip of tea. He looked at Tilly as if he had only just remembered she was there. "How was school?"

"All right," Tilly said, even though it wasn't.

"Made any new friends yet?"

Tilly shook her head. It was too soon. It was hard, starting all over again at a new school with new people. She thought about Ally. She wished she were at the new school with her.

"One more chapter and some more tidying up in the attic, and then I'll stop for today," Dad said. "You OK out here by yourself for a little longer?"

Tilly nodded. "I like it," she said.

"Good." Dad ruffled her hair.

"Don't, Dad!" Tilly ducked away from his hand.

He picked up the tray and went back to the house.

Tilly walked around the garden on the ashy path that went down one side, past rows of raspberry bushes, along under an apple tree and a prickly bit with other fruit bushes, past a stinky compost heap, and then around the other corner and back next to a hedge. What now?

She picked the last rose petals from the bush near the rickety wooden shed. She found an old jam jar on a dusty shelf inside the shed and filled it with water from the outside tap, and squashed in the petals and stirred them with a stick, to make rose scent. She put the scent jar on one of the shelves in the shed, next to a box of nails and a reel of garden string.

She crossed back over the lawn to the metal garden gate and looked through again. The wooden gate opposite had rusty hinges and no latch. It was rotten and falling off the top hinge, and it was slightly open, with a gap just big enough for a slim fox.

Tilly wanted to go through too. But not yet.

Dad was calling her again. "Time to come in! Where are you? Tilly?"

She was glad she was hidden behind the bushes. If he saw her at the gate, she knew he'd say she shouldn't open it. Shouldn't go through. But if he didn't see her, if he didn't say the actual words, maybe she still could.

Just as she turned away, back to the house, she thought she heard something—a snatch of a song, in a thin, reedy voice. Someone did live close by, then, Tilly thought. Someone who might be a new friend, like Ally. Her spine prickled. It was an old-fashioned sort of song, like something Granny would know.

"Hurry up!" Dad was calling.

Tilly followed him into the house.

"When I was sorting through the attic I found something you might like," Dad said.

"What is it?" Tilly asked.

"Come and see."

Tilly went up the stairs behind Dad, along the landing to her bedroom.

An old-fashioned dollhouse sat squarely on the floor in front of the radiator. The walls were made of thin wood, painted a creamy-white color. It had four green-painted bay windows at the front: two upstairs and two downstairs on either side of a green front door. The roof was painted red like tiles, and it had two chimneys at either end.

"Open up the front," Dad said.

Tilly knelt down. The whole of the front of the house opened, so you could get to the rooms inside. There were two bedrooms and a tiny bathroom upstairs, and a kitchen, a living room, and a hall with a tiled floor downstairs. The bedrooms had wallpaper with a pattern of pink climbing roses. There was furniture too: a bed in each room, a wooden kitchen table and chairs, even tiny pots and pans, and a china dog in a tiny wicker basket.

Tilly lifted everything out carefully and blew off the dust, and then put it all back again just as it had been before.

"The back opens up too," Dad said.

Tilly pulled the dollhouse away from the radiator so she could reach around to the back. There were two plain wooden doors with hinges on either side; it wasn't realistic, like the front of the house. She opened the doors and found another set of rooms, all empty except for a family of small dollhouse people: a mother, a father, and a girl, in faded clothes made of felt and with tiny feet in metal shoes. The figures were soft and bendy, so you could make them sit down or straighten them up again, or move their arms as if they were doing things.

"It's very old," Dad said. "It's probably worth something. But it must have belonged to the old lady, and I'm sure she would have wanted you to play with it."

Tilly thought quickly of the girls in her new class at school. None of them would play with dollhouses. Not at their age! She could imagine them saying the words, sneering at her. But they weren't here. They would never know. She made herself stop thinking about them.

"It's lovely," she said. "Can I keep it here, in my room?"

"Of course."

When Dad went downstairs to cook supper, Tilly moved everything around in the dollhouse to make it cozier. She put the father doll in the kitchen. She laid the mother doll on the bed upstairs and sat the girl doll on the chair next to her.

That tune was in her head. The one she'd heard in the garden. The thin notes like a bird's song, but in a girl's clear voice, over and over.

Chapter 4

Tilly sat on the edge of Mom's bed. It was Dad's bed too, but because Mom was still ill she was lying right in the middle, her head on a bank of pillows. Tilly didn't like seeing her like that. Normally, Mom would be rushing about and chatting and singing and doing her drawings for college. Mom was going to be an illustrator when she finished college. *One day*, Mom sighed, as if it was a long way off. When she was better, she was going to turn one of the spare bedrooms into her *studio*. It would be like Dad's study, only nicer, with boxes of paints and pastels and thick, creamy paper.

"What have you been up to?" Mom asked.

Tilly thought about the dollhouse and the garden,

and the rose petal scent, but her voice didn't want to speak and her throat ached.

Dad talked instead. He told Mom about the old dollhouse he'd brought down from the attic for Tilly. "It must have belonged to the old lady who used to live here."

"Miss Helen Sheldon," Mom told Tilly. "I met her once or twice when I was little. She was friends with my mother—that's your Nana. She would be pleased to think you have her dollhouse now."

Mom stroked Tilly's hair and Tilly laid her head down on the bed, close to her. She closed her eyes to smell Mom's special scent. In her head Tilly asked how much longer it was going to be like this, and when Mom could get up again, but her voice wouldn't say the words out loud. There was a lump getting in the way, deep in her throat.

"It won't be forever, sweet pea," Mom whispered into Tilly's hair, as if she knew how much she wanted to know. "Thank you for being so good and patient."

Tilly leaned in close, and she was nearly asleep, lying there while Mom talked with Dad about *arrangements* and the *new chapter*…the words all blurred into one soft hummmmmmm.

Bedtime.

Tilly crouched down to look into the dollhouse windows. Everything was as it should be. She opened up the front, put her hand carefully into the kitchen, and pulled the china dog from his basket. She lifted him up close to look at him properly. He had golden fur and a white bib and a long tail, a bit like the fox. A fox wouldn't sleep in a basket under the kitchen table. Tilly put the dog/fox down on the carpet, outside the dollhouse, looking in.

She climbed into bed. She was sleepy, drifting off almost as soon as she lay down and pulled the blanket up under her ears.

The fox padded across the silent night garden. It placed each foot carefully, stopping every few paces to sniff the air, nose twitching, tail held high, stiff like a brush. It looked up at Tilly's bedroom window.

She sat as still as a stone, watching it back. Her breath

clouded the glass, and in the second it took for her to rub it clear, the fox had gone again.

Tilly climbed back into bed. She thought about the night garden, and the fox. She imagined him squeezing through the metal gate, crossing the grassy path, and slipping around the gap in the old wooden gate, and then what? Next time, Tilly thought, next time I'm going to follow him and see where he goes.

The night-light by her bed cast its soft silver glow over the bedroom. Tilly reached out to look at the clock next to her glass of water. Five to five. Nearly morning. She had expected it to be much earlier: the middle of the night, even. The bark of the fox must have woken her up.

She thought about Mom, pale against the pillow, and the worried crease on Dad's face, in between his dark eyebrows, when he looked at her.

What if Mom didn't get better? What if...?

Tilly pulled furry Little Fox closer. She stroked his head with her cheek.

Chapter 5

T ap tap tap…Dad was busy in his study, typing on the laptop. Tilly listened. The taps made a sort of pattern, a rhythm, as if Dad was playing a tune instead of writing a story. The stories he wrote were for grown-ups and looked boring because there were so many words and no pictures at all. Mom wanted Dad to write a book for children one day, so she could do the illustrations.

Tilly picked at a piece of toast with butter and honey. She was glad it was Saturday and there was no school. But she still wasn't hungry. She took the toast with her out into the garden, and the bird flew down from the tree as if it had been waiting for her.

The garden was waking up in the sun, but it was still

chilly and the grass was wet with dew. Spiders' webs stretched out like fairy nets across the lawn; bigger spiders had made traps by spinning long, sticky strings between the bushes on either side of the path. Tilly stopped to watch a speckledy-brown spider sitting very still in the middle of its web. Spiders were good at waiting.

She went to check on the rose-petal perfume in the shed. The liquid had turned sludgy brown and stank. Tilly chucked it out over the ground next to the rose bush in disgust. She hadn't made rose scent after all.

She wished there was a swing in this garden. Or a tree house or a pond or something more interesting than grass and flower beds and an old vegetable plot. She sat under the tree for a while but it was too cold. She put her hands in her coat pockets and felt something warm and furry. Little Fox! She had forgotten she'd put him in there. She fished him out and sat him on the arm of the bench so he could see the garden. His beady eyes twinkled in the sun.

Tilly looked around quickly. But there was no one there, no one to see and be mean and tell her she was too old to play games like this...

Little Fox didn't like sitting still. Little Fox wanted an adventure. *Come on*, Little Fox said to Tilly. *What are you waiting for?* He led the way to the gate. He could slip through easily, but Tilly needed to undo the latch and open the gate properly. Tilly looked back at the house, once. She could see the windows at the top of one end of the house, but no one was watching.

It was sunny and much warmer on this side of the gate. The hedge sheltered the grassy path. The hedge smelled sweet and strange.

Now where? Tilly asked Little Fox.

Little Fox wanted to explore the grassy path, to see where it went, but then he saw the wooden gate. *This way*, Little Fox said.

Tilly pushed the gate to make a bigger gap, big enough for her, and it squeaked as it inched wider.

"It's another sort of garden," Tilly whispered. But the grass hadn't been cut for a long time. It grew tall and papery, almost higher than Tilly. Big, overgrown clumps of purple flowers were mixed in with the grass, and baby trees were pushing up everywhere, where seeds from a big tree had taken root. *This will be a forest one day*, Tilly thought, *if no one cuts them down.*

Tilly pushed through the long grass. Crickets clicked and jumped ahead of her. Insects hummed and hovered and buzzed. She stopped to watch two ladybugs climbing down a spear-shaped leaf. Farther along, she found a wild brambly patch with a few overripe blackberries still clinging to the prickly branches. Tilly picked and ate the ones she could reach. The juice stained her fingers red: *like blood*, Tilly thought. When Tilly trailed her hand along the top of a rough hedge with gray-green leaves, the smell made her sneeze. *Lavender!* She found a thicket of overgrown roses, with a few last pink flowers and huge thorns along the wiry stems. *Like in* Sleeping Beauty, Tilly thought. *Perhaps there's a castle on the other side.*

This was a wild garden. Anything might happen here. A secret garden, just for her and Little Fox to play in. It was a magic garden, Tilly decided, where the sun always shone and she could be happy and safe, and no one would know she was here. Unless...

She thought about the sound she'd heard the other day, like someone singing. Perhaps it had been a bird after all. There was no sign of anyone else ever coming here. It was all overgrown and wild, as if it had been neglected for a long time. But there was much more to explore. Maybe, if she went farther in, she would find a house and a girl a bit like Ally, who would be her friend.

She'd been out for a long time. Dad would be looking for her.

"We can come back," Tilly whispered to Little Fox. "But we can't tell anyone else. They might try and stop us."

For the first time since they'd moved, Tilly felt a little bit excited.

Chapter 6

It was Saturday again. "We've got shopping to do, Tilly," Dad said.

Tilly put Little Fox on Mom's bedroom windowsill so he could watch over the garden and keep an eye on Mom.

Mom helped Dad make a shopping list. Dad wrote it all down so he wouldn't forget anything or get the wrong things. Tilly didn't listen to their boring list. She had her own things to think about.

The town was busy. It took ages to find a place to park the car. Crowds of people all dressed in the same blue, white, and black sweaters and scarves were pushing and shoving their way toward the rugby field.

"Must be a home match," Dad said. "I'd forgotten."

Tilly and Dad were walking the opposite way of everyone else along the riverside path, moving against the flow. It took a long time to reach the steps leading up to the bridge and the main street.

"What shall we do first? Food or fun?" Dad asked.

"Boring food first," Tilly said. It was best to get it over and done with. That's what Mom would do: supermarket shop first then something for fun, like a café or a bookshop or sometimes both. "Then I know where I want to go for a treat."

The dollhouse shop was in a small street that climbed up a hill to the traffic lights. Tilly stopped to look in the window. It was all lit up with special lights on glass shelves: rows of tiny beds and tables and chairs; a shelf full of food on tiny china plates; garden stuff like benches and flowerpots and a tiny watering can and tools. Tilly looked at the nursery section: a tiny crib on rockers, a cot, a little stroller. There were animals too: a family of kittens in a basket; a black and white collie dog. She liked the little wooden toy box, a bit like her real one, with a hinged lid and everything. Best of all was the tiny dollhouse. A dollhouse to go *inside* a dollhouse! Like Russian dolls, where the dolls go on getting smaller and smaller as you take them apart, until you get to the last teeny one that doesn't open.

Dad was looking at his watch. "How about I leave you here for ten minutes or so, Tilly, and then come back to get you? Then I can take care of a few things I need to do."

Tilly nodded. Mom would have enjoyed coming right in with her and looking at everything: the special wallpaper and the electric light sets and the rows of tiny dolls, and the houses themselves. But Dad would fidget and be bored. He would say how everything was too expensive.

Tilly watched him going off down the hill. Suddenly, the street seemed too big and busy, and she was too small and alone. She pushed the shop door open and went inside.

The shop lady smiled from behind the counter. She didn't say anything, and she went back to shuffling papers and writing things down.

Tilly began to relax. First she looked at the rows of dollhouses on a big shelf on one side of the shop, then she crossed over to where there were more cabinets full of stuff like in the window, and then she studied the families. It was important to get the size right. Most of these people were too big for Tilly's dollhouse. That was because her dollhouse was very old.

She thought about what Mom had told her. The dollhouse was older than Mom or Granny even. It had belonged to the old lady called Miss Sheldon who had lived in the house before them. It had been Miss Sheldon's dollhouse when *she* was a girl, a long, long time ago. She hadn't had any children of her own. And that's how Mom, Dad, and Tilly had come to live in her house. Miss Sheldon died when she was nearly one hundred years old. She had left the house to Mom in her will.

Tilly only had enough money for one thing from her list. She went to the window to choose. The lady was watching her now. Tilly took a long time to decide. The tiny dollhouse was best of all, but it cost too much. She picked up the cradle instead.

"You made a good choice," the

lady said as she handed Tilly her change. "I love that cradle too. I like the way it actually rocks." She wrapped it up in pale pink tissue paper and put the package into a blue paper bag. "Have you got a baby to put in it?" the lady asked.

"Not yet," Tilly whispered.

Now she didn't know what to do. The door jangled again as she opened it and stepped out into the street. She looked up and then down the street, but there was no sign of Dad. He'd said ten minutes, but it seemed much longer than that. She was glad no one spoke to her or asked her what she was doing there. She felt too small all by herself in town, even though lots of the girls in her new class wouldn't have thought twice about it. Harriet, Lucy, and Simone came to town by themselves *every* Saturday, they said.

She didn't want to think about those girls. She imagined meeting them now, and the way they'd smile and stare at her clothes and toss their hair and giggle to each other. They'd think she was weird, still being interested in *dollhouses* at her age!

Dad was running up the hill at last, laden with bags, and smiling.

"Sorry! I got carried away!" Dad said. "Got what you wanted?"

Tilly nodded.

"Come on then, before the parking meter runs out."

They jogged together back to the car. This end of town wasn't so busy, now that the match was in full swing. Every so often the roar of thousands of voices echoed up from the riverside field as someone scored.

Tilly shoved the paper bag deep in her pocket to keep it safe.

She climbed into the front seat while Dad stowed all the bags in the trunk. Dad was in a good mood. He chattered all the way home about the books he'd found in the thrift store. Her hand curled around the package in her pocket, feeling the small wooden shape nestling in the paper.

"We should have bought a get-better-soon present for Mom," Tilly said.

Dad looked at her. "Flowers?" he said. "What do you think? I can stop at the florist on the corner if it's still open. You could run in and choose her some."

Dad stopped the car just outside the flower shop. "Here," he said to Tilly. He gave her some money.

Tilly looked at all the buckets of flowers on the

pavement outside the shop. Then she went inside to see what was there. She picked out a bunch of pink and creamy-white flowers, and the florist wrapped them up and tied a ribbon around them. "Someone's birthday?" she asked. "She's going to be very pleased."

Tilly didn't say anything. She just smiled and handed over Dad's money and went back out to the car with the change in one hand and the flowers in the other.

"That'll do the trick," Dad said. "And we'll make tea and sandwiches for the three of us when we get home."

Little Fox was bored. He wanted an adventure. *Can't we go back to the magic garden?* he asked Tilly when she picked him up off the windowsill.

It's getting dark, Tilly said. *It's cold outside now.*

So? I've got fur and you can put on your coat! Little Fox said.

Dad and Mom were deep in conversation. Dad was eating his way through the pile of sandwiches. The pink and white flowers were in a big glass vase on the table. Mom had said they were *truly beautiful, the perfect choice.*

Tilly slid down off the windowsill. "Can I go and play?" she asked Dad.

He nodded. He didn't ask *where*. He didn't say *not outside*.

Downstairs, Tilly put on her coat. She slipped her feet into rain boots. She put Little Fox in her pocket. She opened the back door and went into the garden. Birds were flying high in the blue-dark sky, calling to each other. Lots of birds, flying together in a V-shape, with one bird leading the way, as if they were traveling a long distance.

It was nearly dark, but once you were outside, your eyes got used to it and it wasn't really dark at all.

Hurry up! Little Fox said.

They crossed the grass. The little bird scolded from the tree—*tut tut!*

Tilly opened the gate, crossed the grassy path, and squeezed around the wooden door into the magic garden.

Chapter 7

Tilly put Little Fox down on the ground at the foot of a big tree, where the trunk turned into twisting roots and dead leaves had piled up in between to make a soft sitting place. Tilly settled down to think.

A blackbird flew over, calling out its warning cry. Above her, high in the tree, a robin began to sing. Tilly remembered that other song, from before. But there was no sign of anyone here today. Just her and the wild birds, and maybe a fox, hidden somewhere.

What now?

I'm going to make a den, Tilly thought. A secret place where I can come whenever I want to, and no one can find me.

Where would be a good place for a den? There was

the deep bramble thicket, where something had already burrowed a way through, close to the ground, making a tunnel. It looked dry and secret, except that the *something* might still be living in there. And possibly it was a tunnel to get to somewhere else—a sort of animal road.

Tilly thought some more. She liked sitting here, right under this tree. It felt safe and quiet and hidden. This was a perfect place. If she dragged some big branches over and leaned them against the trunk, she could weave other stuff like dry grass and twigs in between the branches. She could decorate the inside with moss and have a log for a table and a smaller one for a chair. It would be good to have a doorway that could be opened and shut. The tree would shelter her, with its big, spreading branches like arms. Tilly could see it all clearly in her mind.

She started to explore the garden, looking for things for her den. She went farther than she'd been before. The garden was huge. There were woods at one end. But there was no sign of a house or a girl.

Under the trees, along a crumbling stone wall, she found lots of dead branches. She shoved and dragged them back to the tree. Some of the logs were too weak and they broke into useless small pieces, but soon she had enough to start piling them up into a wigwam leaning against the tree, to make a base for the walls. She gathered handfuls of dry grass to begin weaving through, in and out, over and under. It took a long time. Her hands were cold. She crept inside her den and sat in the middle, arms hugging her knees, and looked out through the doorway.

The garden was rustling and stirring, as if the night-time creatures were waking up.

In her den, Tilly felt safe. *Keep out!* she said fiercely in her head. *This is my den!*

Mine too! Little Fox said.

Tilly stroked his furry head against her cheek. He felt

cold. "Time to go back," she whispered to Little Fox. She held him tight in her hand as she squeezed through the door gap and walked past the old lavender hedge, back along the path they'd made before, when they first explored the long grass. This time, the crickets were silent. A blackbird flew away, calling its warning cry: *spink spink!* It was completely dark now.

Through the wooden gate, across the path, back through the metal gate, and onto the lawn went Tilly and Little Fox. Tilly's boots left prints in the damp grass. The lights from the house windows shone out, casting pale gold squares over the garden. Dad had forgotten to close the curtains. Tilly crossed the squares like stepping stones, all the way back to the kitchen.

Tilly pulled off her boots and hung up her coat.

Tap tap tap came the sound from Dad's study. Tilly padded upstairs. She went from room to room, pulling the curtains tight, keeping in the light.

Mom's door was ajar. Tilly crept in.

Mom was listening to the radio. She turned and

smiled at Tilly. "You're freezing!" She kissed Tilly's cheek. "What have you been doing?"

"Exploring outside," Tilly said. She put Little Fox down on the bed.

"Ah," Mom said. She sighed. "I can't wait till I'm up and about, and everything can go back to normal." She smiled at Tilly. "Well, not quite *normal*, perhaps!" She reached out her hand to stroke Little Fox. "He's getting a bit threadbare. And he's all muddy and damp!"

"I took him out to the garden with me," Tilly said.

"It's a beautiful garden. It will be even better in the spring," Mom said. "You can invite some friends over to play in it with you when it's warmer."

Tilly didn't tell her that she didn't have any *friends* to invite. Not yet.

She didn't tell her about the other garden, either. The secret one.

The *tap tap tapping* stopped. Dad came to the bedroom door. "Want to help me cook supper, Tilly?"

Tilly left Little Fox to dry out on Mom's bed. She went downstairs with Dad, to make pasta sauce. She was getting good at cooking. She could do pancakes and pasta and French toast now.

Chapter 8

It was Sunday bedtime. Tilly pulled back the curtain to look outside. The moon was rising: a big, full, golden saucer in the blue-black sky. She turned off the lamp next to her bed so she could see outside better. The garden seemed to be extra still, waiting for something to happen.

Tilly climbed back into bed and curled up under the white blanket, one hand on Little Fox. She thought about her den in the secret garden. The way the moonlight would make shadow patterns on the dead leaves.

Imagine! Little Fox whispered in her ear. *Imagine being there now.*

The moon had moved high up in the sky. The clouds had cleared, and now the sky was scattered with stars. The night garden was full of sounds. An owl hooted. Something scurried through dry leaves under a bush. In her white fleece robe, Tilly moved like a ghost across the grass, under the tree, between the bushes, and through the gate. Across the grassy path she went, through the wooden door into the secret garden. Her feet left hardly a trace on the moonlit grass. The wind barely moved her long hair, loose around her shoulders.

And there, right in front of her, was the fox.

The fox she'd seen before, through her bedroom window.

She stopped short; the fox stopped too. They stared at each other, girl and fox.

The fox looked deep into her eyes. The fox's eyes were a deep gold color, like the jewels on Granny's necklace made from real amber. A tingle went down Tilly's spine. She took a small step forward. The fox turned, lifted one padded paw, and started to walk again. It

44

stopped, looked over its shoulder, as if it was waiting for Tilly to follow.

Everything looked different in the nighttime garden. The moonlight made every blade of grass, every edge of twig and leaf shine silver.

Tilly followed the fox. It padded softly through the long, silver grass, along the path Tilly had made, toward the tree and the den. It stopped. It turned around. Its ears were pricked up high, its eyes glinting in the moonlight. Its breath made misty puffs in the cold air. Tilly was so close up she could see the way its sides went in and out as it breathed. Its tongue lolled out of its mouth, panting.

Something soft whooshed past Tilly and made her jump. She turned; a white owl glided over the garden.

The owl swooped down, and there was a shrill shriek and the owl took off again, something small and furry in its claws.

Tilly shivered.

When she turned back, the fox had gone.

She stared at her den. She went closer to see better.

Threaded in and out of the dried old grass she'd used to

cover the wigwam of branches was a string of dark red rose hips, like beads on a necklace.

Tilly pulled one of the rose hips out and crushed it in her hand. Inside were yellow seeds and a kind of fluff that made her skin itch. She looked around, in case someone was watching her. But there was no one there. It was an odd feeling, that someone else had been here and found her den, and put the rose hips there. Who would do such a thing?

The girl, of course!

The girl who sang that old-fashioned song…

Tilly crawled inside the den, and sat down with her back against the tree trunk and hugged her knees. Her feet felt the rough texture of the leaves and the peaty soil where leaves had rotted down to make earth. She sat there for ages. Perhaps, if she waited long enough, the girl would come back…

What was that?

For a brief second, she thought she heard something: a woman's voice, faint, calling a name.

Tilly peered into the dark garden. The voice seemed to be carried on the wind, from a long way off. Tilly crept forward to listen.

All she heard now were the rustlings and stirrings of a creature rummaging through dead leaves, and then a moth fluttering close to her ear, ruffling the still air with its fast-beating wings.

She must have imagined it. The sound was probably just in her head, the way a tune you've heard gets stuck sometimes and plays on, over and over, whether you like it or not.

Something else rustled. Tilly held her breath and watched.

The fox was back. She could see him now, standing still, his dark red-brown fur tinged with silver, his breath making puffs of smoke on the frosty air.

The fox turned, looked at her, and started walking slowly through the long grass.

"Wait," Tilly said. "Where are you going?" She shivered, suddenly afraid. She was cold all over, cold to her very bones. Instantly, she knew she must get back inside, into the house. What was she thinking, coming out into the garden in the middle of the night, all alone, in the cold, with bare feet and only a bathrobe?

She started to run.

Chapter 9

Tilly woke up. She was in her bed, snuggled under the white blanket. Her feet were toasty-warm; just the tip of her nose felt cold. The bedroom was already light. She reached across for the little alarm clock on the bedside table. Not quite time to get up. But it was Monday, and that meant it was a school morning. The thought brought with it the feeling in her belly that came every school morning, these days, like eels squirming around.

Automatically, her hand reached out for Little Fox for comfort. But he wasn't under her pillow or tucked under the blanket next to her as usual. Perhaps he'd fallen out of bed? Tilly looked down, she felt around with her hand under the bed, but he wasn't there either. She tried to remember going to sleep last night, but instead other memories started to flood her mind.

Pad pad pad...Dad's footsteps came along the landing.

"Time to get up for school, Tilly." He padded into the bathroom and shut the door.

Tilly lay in bed listening to the sound of water swooshing in the bathroom. The bedroom radiator clunked and clinked as water gurgled along the pipes. Even if she waited longer, it would still be cold in the bedroom. It never warmed up properly.

She climbed out of bed. She touched her dressing gown, hanging neatly on the back of the door; was that a tiny yellow seed, caught on a thread on the sleeve?

Tilly slowly got dressed in her school clothes. She went to see if Mom was awake.

The door was slightly ajar. Tilly peeped around. Mom was lying on her side, eyes shut, breathing deeply. Tilly watched for a moment; the mound of Mom's body under the white blanket, the way it moved slightly up and down in time with her steady breathing. A strand of

Mom's hair had escaped and lay on the pillow in a dark curl like a question mark.

"Go and wash your hands and face, Tilly." Dad touched her head lightly as he came past her into the bedroom...He smelled of toothpaste. "Then come downstairs for breakfast. Let Mom sleep a little longer."

Mom didn't do anything *but* sleep, it seemed to Tilly. How much sleep could one person possibly need? And why wasn't she getting any better? Instead, she just seemed to be getting worse.

In the kitchen, Tilly nibbled a corner of toast and honey. Dad was in a rush, making her sandwiches for lunch, brushing her school shoes, making coffee for himself. Tilly swung her legs while she thought about Mom, back and forth. "She's never going to get better, is she?" Tilly whispered, but so softly that Dad didn't hear.

"Coat, bag, books," Dad said. "Got everything? Time to go."

Tilly slid off the stool and went to get her coat from the hook in the hall. She picked up her bag and put in her lunch box. Dad opened the front door, and a swirl of wind whipped a trail of dry, dead leaves into the house.

"Hold tight," Dad said. "We're going to get blown

all the way to school today." They set off, Tilly half running, half skipping to keep up with his big strides.

Dad left her at the playground gate. It looked like such a long way to the classroom door, like crossing acres of wasteland, with all sorts of dangers to get past.

Harriet, Simone, and Lucy were standing in a huddle near the jungle gym. They stopped talking to watch her run past. She kept on running until she was at the classroom door and nearly bumped into her teacher.

"Hold on, Tilly!" Mrs. Almond said. "Don't worry; you're not late. The bell hasn't rung yet."

Tilly hung up her coat and put her lunch box on the cart. The classroom felt warm compared to outside. She walked over to the reading corner to choose a book to read. She searched the shelves and then through the box on the floor, which had the books too big to fit on the shelves. She found a book with a picture of a fox on the cover, but the inside looked boring; just a list of facts.

"Are you looking for something in particular?" Mrs. Almond asked Tilly.

Tilly shook her head. She took a book called *Arctic Spring* and sat on the bean bag, slowly turning the pages.

The pictures were beautiful. There was one page with an Arctic fox whose fur changed from brown or gray to snowy white when winter came.

After attendance, Mrs. Almond told the class about a visitor who was coming to the school after break. "She's a writer," Mrs. Almond said. "Like Tilly's father, only she writes children's books." Mrs. Almond smiled at Tilly.

Tilly saw the way Lucy looked at Harriet. Harriet whispered something to Simone.

The eels in Tilly's stomach squirmed some more. She felt sick.

She closed her eyes.

For a moment, it cut out all the sounds too. It was just Tilly, all by herself, in the dark. And then she saw something else, just a movement to begin with, and a shadow that became a shape, and the shape was an animal, moving into view: a fox. The fox looked straight at Tilly, and then trotted on, bold as anything.

Tilly opened her eyes. The fox had gone, but the feeling inside her had changed. Suddenly brave, she stared right back at Lucy and Harriet and Simone. They stopped whispering. One by one, they each went back to reading their books.

It was recess. Tilly dreaded going out to the playground. She took a long time to put on her coat, lingered at the restroom on the way out. If only she still had Ally with her. They'd always been together at her old school.

The three girls from her class were sitting together, huddled tightly on the bench under the tree, whispering and laughing. They watched her come out of the door.

Tilly took a deep breath, stood still, closed her eyes. She tried to imagine the fox. She waited.

The fox nosed its way around the side of the building, past the trash cans and the caretaker's shed, and this time he was white as snow, like the Arctic fox in the picture. His eyes were bright and he lifted each foot up carefully, deliberately. He bared his teeth and she saw they were razor sharp.

Someone pushed into Tilly from behind. Startled, she opened her eyes. Two boys from kindergarten were already racing off. They hadn't meant to hurt her, it was just that she was standing in the way of their chasing each other and they weren't looking where they were going.

Tilly looked at the girls on the bench under the tree. Lucy had shifted along a little, away from the others. Harriet and Simone were swinging their legs, as if they were bored. Tilly walked slowly past them, and they didn't seem to notice her. They didn't giggle or whisper or say anything.

She went to watch the jump rope game at the other side of the playground. The custodian was holding one end of the rope, and Mrs. Almond turned the other. The rope swished down on the playground in a rhythm. A line of boys and girls took turns to jump.

Mrs. Almond smiled at her. "Do you want to join in, Tilly?"

Tilly shook her head. She was fine just watching for now. She knew the rhyme they were chanting from her old school.

The writer who came into the classroom after break had very short gray hair and big silver earrings. She looked like someone's granny until she laughed, and then she looked just like a little girl, Tilly thought. She read them a funny story about a girl and then she said they could each make up their own story, about anything they wanted.

Only Tilly couldn't think what to write. When she closed her eyes, for a second the fox was there, watching her. It was the real red-brown fox this time, not the snowy Arctic one from the picture. Tilly didn't want to write about the fox; he was private and special, just for her. She didn't want to share him with anyone else.

Tilly opened her eyes. Everyone seemed to be busy, writing or drawing. She stared at her empty page. The writer lady smiled at Tilly. "It's the hardest thing, starting off, isn't it?" she said. "Just write any old words down on the blank page to begin with, and after a while, the story will arrive. You just have to let it come when it's ready. Like a shy animal."

Tilly's story was so shy it wanted

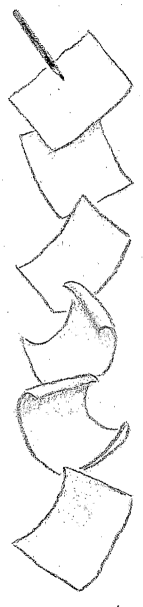

to stay hidden in the forest where no one could see it. She thought about a forest for a while. She imagined a little bird, a wren with a pointed-up tail, hidden in a prickly tree. Then she imagined a cat. In her mind, the cat was fat and getting fatter. It was much too fat to catch the bird. All it wanted to do all day was sleep. The cat stared at her with its round golden eyes and droopy white whiskers. It started to purr.

Mrs. Almond let them continue writing their stories after lunch, and they drew pictures to go with the words until it was time to go home.

Dad was waiting for her on the playground, on his own, away from the crowd of moms, who were mostly all talking and laughing together. Tilly walked slowly across to Dad.

"Did you have a nice day?" he said.

"We wrote stories," Tilly said. "And Mrs. Almond let us carry on for the whole afternoon."

"Sounds like my favorite sort of day!" Dad said. "Do you want to tell me about your story?"

"Not yet," Tilly said. "Only that it's about a cat. A very fat cat."

"Is it a greedy cat?" Dad asked. "Does it eat dough-nuts and candy all day?"

"No," Tilly said. "It's fat and tired because it's going to have kittens."

"Ah," Dad said. He didn't ask any more questions.

"How's Mom?" Tilly said as they walked along the pavement.

"Very tired," Dad said. The worried frown came back on his face.

Tilly was quiet after that, all the way home.

Chapter 10

Tilly was looking for Little Fox. She couldn't find him anywhere. She crept into Mom's room so as not to disturb her, and searched on the bed. She checked behind the curtains, in case he was on the windowsill. Mom stayed fast asleep, propped up against the pillows, even when Tilly stood right up close. The stray strand of dark hair curled across the pillow and Tilly smoothed it back, and still Mom slept on.

Tilly went along the hallway to her own room for another look under her bed. There was lots of fluff and a dried up roly-poly, but no Little Fox. He wasn't in the kitchen. She even looked in the room where Dad wrote his books, although why Little Fox would be in there she couldn't imagine. The table was piled high with pieces of paper, Dad's computer perched precariously at one side. Transparent plastic boxes full of typed pages from his old manuscripts covered most of the carpet. All around the walls were shelves of books, going from the floor right to the ceiling. Some of them, Tilly knew, were old books, left behind in the house like the furniture and pictures and the dollhouse. Dad had been very excited when he found them. They had dusty old covers. Some even had black and white drawings inside, even though they were books for grown-ups. And why shouldn't grown-ups have stories with pictures?

She found a stack of old pictures leaned against one of the shelves: framed photographs of people they didn't know. There was one of a girl with long hair, in a buttoned-up coat, holding something in her lap— Tilly peered at the grainy old photo a bit closer: a kitten, perhaps? Or a small puppy? The girl stared back at Tilly, a sort of half-smile on her lips. Perhaps it was the old lady who had lived here when she was ten or eleven, Tilly thought. It was nice to think she might have looked like this once.

Tilly put the picture back with the others.

There was no sign of Little Fox anywhere. She gave up the search.

Tilly went into her bedroom and knelt down in front of the dollhouse. The father doll was sitting in the armchair near the fire. She moved the mother doll and put her in the other chair, and put the little girl doll upstairs in her room. Tilly had already made a pink cover for the bed, to match the roses on the wallpaper. She was going to make lots more things.

She remembered, suddenly, the little wooden cradle she had bought at the dollhouse shop. She'd forgotten all about it! She ran along the moss green strip of carpet and down the stairs to the hall, where her coat was hanging on its peg. She checked the pockets. The paper bag from the shop was there, but the cradle wasn't. It must have fallen out when she'd been playing outside.

Tilly put on her coat and went to fetch her boots from the kitchen. She yanked the back door behind her. It was freezing outside! She pulled her hood up. Tilly retraced her steps around the garden, trying to remember exactly where she walked last time she played out here. Perhaps Little Fox would be in the same place as the wooden cradle?

But she didn't find either.

She looked back at the house, at the closed doors and blank windows. Dad was busy with something, not looking out of the window, so he wouldn't be able to see her. Tilly ran between the two silver bushes and opened the gate, pulled it shut behind her, ran across the grass lane to the wooden gate, and squeezed into the magic garden.

It was getting dark. *Dusk.* Tilly loved that word and the other one: *twilight.* She trod carefully through the tall grass, then along past the lavender hedge and the bramble patch, toward the oak tree. Her heart pattered against her ribs suddenly. There was her den, waiting for her. But what would she find this time?

It all looked different in the evening light. But the rose hips were still there, faded and a bit dried up, woven into the grass. She hadn't imagined it, then. And there was more: someone had definitely been here. She looked over her shoulder quickly, to check again if she was being watched.

In front of her, laid carefully on the ground, a spiral of white stones wound around into the den, a bit like a maze.

Tilly crouched down to peer closer; the stones were all different sizes, pieces of gray-white flint, and someone had arranged them on purpose, so that the stones got smaller as you went farther in. She wriggled through the narrow gap between the lattice of branches, following the stones.

Where the stone trail ended, in the middle of the den, perched on the log table, was the little dollhouse cradle.

Tilly turned around quickly to see if the girl was there, watching her. Because it must be the singing girl who had found the cradle and left it for her, like that, wasn't it? And she must have made the stone spiral, to show her where to look, guiding her in.

But no one was here now.

She picked up the cradle. It nestled, small and cold, on her palm. It wasn't broken, or even muddy from the ground. She slipped it carefully into her pocket, well tucked in. *Thank you!* she said in her head, to the girl, or whoever it was who had found it for her. And then she thought, I should leave something here, to say thank you *properly*.

She rummaged in her pockets. Right at the bottom of one, covered in fluff, she found an old hair pin in the shape of a butterfly. She could leave that. It wasn't much—it was a bit old and rusty at the edges—but it was still pretty.

Tilly settled down, her back against the tree trunk, peering out through the gap into the night garden.

A twig snapped. Something rustled in the bramble patch. Was she going to see the girl at last?

Tilly sat very still and waited. Her eyes adjusted to the half-light. Like an animal, she thought. I'm just like one of the other creatures living in the wild garden.

Outside, the dark shadow solidified and became an actual animal. The fox was less than three feet away, his head dipped low, nose sniffing the ground where her boots had flattened the grass as she crawled into the den. Could he smell her? Almost immediately, the fox slipped back into the shadowy undergrowth. She had been *that close* to him this time. Her own real, wild fox! Close enough for her to see how thin he was, to make out the line of his bony rib cage, and notice his moth-eaten, scraggy tail. The fox looked hungry. Hungry and even ill, perhaps.

In the far distance, Tilly heard a voice calling her name.

The fox must have heard it too. That's why he'd disappeared again so soon.

Dad was calling her. Quickly, she crawled out of the den and picked her way back through the grass, around the gate, back to their regular garden before he could discover where she'd really been hiding.

She ran across the lawn to the back door.

"There you are!" Dad ruffled her hair. "What are you doing out here in the dark? I thought the night garden had swallowed you up!"

"I was looking for Little Fox," Tilly said. "He's lost."

"He's probably in the house somewhere," Dad said. "We'll look together later." Back in the warm kitchen, he helped Tilly tug off her boots. "You're going to need new ones soon!" Dad said. "You're growing up fast, Til!"

Tilly put her arms around his middle. His woolly sweater was warm and scratchy against her face.

"Now. Supper," Dad said. "Pasta again or French toast?"

"Pancakes," Tilly said.

Tilly fetched the little cradle from her coat pocket and took it upstairs with her. She opened the front of the dollhouse. She couldn't decide where to put it. She tried it in the mom and dad's room, and then next to the single bed in the little girl's bedroom, and then downstairs. It didn't seem to fit anywhere. In the end, she left it in the attic room, under the eaves, by itself. She touched it with her fingertip, to set it rocking.

Outside, the fox called its strange, harsh cry into the night.

All night, Tilly twisted and turned in her bed, worrying even in her dreams. In her sleep, she reached out her hand for the comforting softness of Little Fox, but her hand stayed empty.

Chapter 11

It was Christmas Eve.

"Do you want to come with me to choose the Christmas tree?" Dad asked Tilly at breakfast time. "Soon as I get back from shopping?"

"Yes please," Tilly said. Inside her, a little bubble of happiness was growing. There was no school because of the holidays, and they were going to have Christmas at home, and Mom was going to come downstairs and have a bed on the sofa, so she could be there too. Tilly had made a list of presents she wanted, because Dad was having to do all the shopping and getting-ready-for-Christmas things without Mom this year.

Once Dad had gone off to town, Tilly went upstairs.

Mom was awake, propped up against the pillows. She smiled at Tilly. "What are you going to do today, Til?"

"I'm making more things for the dollhouse. Pictures for the walls and some rugs and things for the bedroom, and a tiny Christmas stocking."

"Why don't you bring it all in here?" Mom said. "We can chat while you're busy working."

Tilly brought Mom's sewing basket upstairs. She pulled out odds and ends of fabric. Mom helped her choose which pieces would be best for each thing. She showed Tilly how to sew tiny, neat stitches to hem the edges so they didn't fray.

"How will you make the pictures for the walls?" Mom asked. "Maybe you could cut things out of a magazine, or print some tiny pictures off the computer."

"I'm going to draw them," Tilly said. "I want them to be like the old pictures that belonged to this house."

"Miss Sheldon's pictures?"

"Yes."

Tilly had worked it all out. She had found some thin pieces of wood that she could cut to the right size and colored pencils to draw with. It was tricky, making it all tiny enough to fit the dollhouse.

"I've got some gold pens somewhere," Mom said. "You could make the edges look like old-fashioned gold frames. Take a look in the bottom drawer in that chest under the window."

Tilly pulled out the heavy drawer. It smelled musty and old and delicious. She found the pens and some thin brushes and paints which would be perfect, and more fabrics and thick paper in rolls. "It's your artist's drawer!" Tilly laughed.

"It's my secret box of delights!" Mom said.

"You could do some drawing in bed," Tilly said. "I'll get everything for you, so you can just stay there."

Mom looked sad. "My head hurts too much, Tilly. I need some sleep, really. But you can stay here quietly working if you like, until Dad gets back."

Choosing a tree was one of the best things ever, Tilly thought. The courtyard at the back of the garden center was filled with trees, like a strange forest. It smelled of Christmas: pine and spice and something she couldn't quite name.

"We can have a tall tree for the first time ever," Dad said. "What with our high ceilings and all."

But Tilly had already found the one she wanted: a small tree with perfectly balanced branches, dark green needles, and a straight tip at the top which would be just right for hanging the star. "This is the one," she said.

It was already dark when they got home. Tilly went through the house, switching on the lights in all the rooms while Dad went out to the garden shed to search for a pot for the tree to stand in.

"I'll go and find the decorations," Dad said. "They'll be in the attic in one of those boxes."

Usually, it was Mom and Tilly who decorated the tree together, and Mom put on her CD of Christmas carols to make it feel special, and for Tilly it was the magical moment when Christmas really started.

After supper, while Dad did the washing up, Tilly went back to the living room. The tree was standing there, bare and mysterious. For just a second, Tilly thought how beautiful it was without any decorations at all. She opened the box and took out the first ornaments, and the star, and the birds made of feathers, which had been a present from Granny one year, and started to hang them on the branches. She hung up the glass bell; it tinkled when she touched it and swung softly, like a real bell. She unwrapped the tissue around the old glass ornaments, silver and pink and gold, which had been handed down, one generation to the next, from Nana and Granny to Mom and Dad. She hung them all up, so they spun and shone in the light. Last of all she fished the tree lights out of the bottom of the box and draped them around in a spiral, like Mom usually did.

Tilly turned off all the lights except the ones on the tree. Shadows moved across the wall, tracing the shape of the branches. Tilly sat on the sofa and breathed in the smell of pine forest. She shivered with excitement.

At bedtime, Tilly hung up her Christmas stocking at the bottom of her bed. She knelt down and opened up the dollhouse so she could put the tiny stocking she had made earlier on the end of the pink bed cover in the girl's bedroom. She straightened one of the tiny gold-framed pictures she'd hung up earlier in the day, her favorite one, the portrait of the girl with long hair. She closed the dollhouse door and set the china dog/fox back in his place outside.

Tilly climbed into bed and snuggled under the blanket. Her feet were cold. Mom and Dad's voices drifted along the landing, rising and falling as they talked to each other. She heard Dad go downstairs to the kitchen.

It was so hard to get to sleep. She got out of bed again and went to the window. It was too dark to see anything; the moon had not yet risen. She thought she heard the bark of the fox. It was as if it was calling her... *come out... come and see the garden this magical Christmas night...*

She climbed back into bed. She turned her pillow over to find a cool place for her hot head. She wished Little Fox were here, soft against her cheek. She thought about the fox and the garden and the mysterious girl...and as she drifted toward sleep at last, she was already dreaming...

Chapter 12

When the moon first rose above the trees it looked huge, like an enormous silver saucer. It spilled its strange, silvery light over the grass and trees, as if it was showing the way across one garden, through the gate, across to the other garden, and all the way to Tilly's den.

Under the trees it seemed darker than before. The trees seemed bigger than ever, and there were more of them, as if a forest had sprung up. It smelled of pine and spice, that mysterious, delicious Christmas smell. Tilly crept under the trees, her white dressing gown wrapped tightly around her, her feet in pink slippers feeling their way over the frosted grass and dead leaves and bits of broken branches.

Ahead of her, something glowed with a soft light—not moonlight but something else, a light that flickered and moved. Candles, Tilly suddenly realized. Small candles in silver candle holders attached to the lower branches of a small fir tree next to her den. She stopped and looked, mesmerized by how beautiful it was.

She could hear something. A humming sound, as if someone was singing under their breath while they were busy doing something, and then a girl's voice, laughing, called out softly, "Tilly! Merry Christmas!"

Tilly went forward, her heart fluttering with excitement. She pulled back the bracken and grass from the door of the den, so she could crawl in.

In the flickering light sat a girl about Tilly's age, with long hair, dressed in a green woollen coat with a velvet collar, and brown laced-up boots, smiling at her.

"Oh!" Tilly whispered. "At last! I've sooo wanted to see you!"

"Come on in!" The girl patted the ground next to her. "Sit yourself down."

Tilly hardly dared breathe. She crept inside, trembling. She sat down next to the girl. She smiled shyly.

The girl smiled back.

The den had been transformed. Like the decorations on a Christmas tree, the branches of the den were hung with silver ornaments and a pink glass bell, and a small silver trumpet which spun around, slowly, shining in the light from the candle on the small table in the middle.

"Do you like it?" the girl asked.

"It's beautiful!" Tilly said. "Thank you!"

"You're welcome," the girl said in her old-fashioned voice. She started unwrapping things from the basket by her side: slices of cake, russet apples, two small oranges, a thick slice of meat bread, and cheese wrapped in a piece of cloth.

"A midnight feast!" Tilly said.

"Of course. A feast for Christmas Eve. Are you hungry?"

Tilly didn't think she was. But the cake looked delicious, and she nibbled at the thick white icing, and then she had an apple, and a sliver of cheese…

"We could give the leftovers to the fox," Tilly said, when they had both had enough. "Do you know about the fox?"

The girl laughed. "Yes! Of course. It's still getting used to you, though. Foxes are shy creatures."

They put the meat and the cheese and the rest of the bread outside the den and waited for the fox to appear. They waited for ages. Tilly began to feel cold, shivery.

"Perhaps the fox won't come while we're here," Tilly said. "And I'd better go home soon, in any case."

"I've seen you in the garden lots of times," the girl said. "But you've never spotted me before, have you?"

"I've heard you singing," Tilly said. "But you're very good at hiding. Is this your garden, then? Did you mind about me making the den?"

"Of course not! I helped you to make it even better. Didn't you notice?"

"The rose hips and things?"

"Yes, and I put more bracken and grass and moss over the branches, to make it stronger and more rainproof. You can sit in here when it's raining and it hardly comes in at all."

"How many times have you been here?" Tilly asked.

"Lots. I bring a book sometimes and read. Or make things, like necklaces, from berries and things I find. Or just hide quietly, so I can watch the birds and the animals and no one can see me."

"Did you find the butterfly clip?" Tilly said shyly. "It was to say thank you, for finding the little cradle I lost. It was you, wasn't it?"

"Yes!" The girl turned her head, so Tilly could see the butterfly in her red-brown hair. It glinted in the candlelight, not rusty at all anymore. "I really wanted to keep the cradle…it was so pretty. But I knew it must be yours. And the clip is pretty too."

"Will you be here tomorrow?" Tilly asked. "Can I come and play?"

"Maybe. Maybe not," the girl said. "I come and I go. It's time for me to go now!"

"Me too," Tilly said. She wriggled through the door after the girl, out into the garden. It was darker than ever. The wind must have blown out all the candles on the fir tree. Clouds covered the moon.

"Good-bye! Merry Christmas! See you soon!" The girl was already running off into the night. She turned once, briefly, to wave at Tilly, before she disappeared under the trees.

I forgot to ask her name, Tilly thought. Next time...

It was early morning. Tilly turned over in her bed. As she moved her feet, she heard the rustle of the Christmas stocking. She moved her toes again, to feel the delicious weight of it. She reached out for the clock on the bed-side table. Six o'clock. It was still too early to wake up Mom and Dad, to go rushing through to their room to open her presents.

She turned on the bedside light, reached down, and pulled the stocking up so she could see it properly. It was stuffed to the top with small packages all wrapped up in pink shiny paper with silver stars. Tilly pulled at the top one, undid one end, and then put it back, suddenly guilty. She must wait for morning.

The bubble of happiness inside her was growing bigger and stronger. It was Christmas. Mom would be coming downstairs for once, to be with her and Dad all day. And she had a new friend at last. A girl a little like her, and a little bit like Ally...

Tilly lay quietly in bed, waiting for the day to begin.

Chapter 13

Tilly lay on the rug in the living room, staring up at the Christmas tree. It was nearly teatime. Mom dozed on the sofa, her Christmas present book from Dad open by her side.

If Tilly squinted her eyes, the tree lights looked magical; they shone and danced like the real candles that Dad had lit all along the fireplace.

Tilly kept thinking about the den and the fir tree and the girl. It was too hard to keep it all a secret today.

"There's a girl living next door, in that big garden..." she started to tell Mom.

"Hmmm." Mom made a soft sighing sound.

Tilly looked up at her. She waited for Mom to say something about the girl. Mom sighed again and turned over slightly. Her eyes were closed.

"Are you asleep?" Tilly asked eventually.

Mom didn't say anything. Tilly watched the way her body went up and down, steadily, as she breathed deeply. Yes, Mom was fast asleep.

Never mind. They had had a perfect day together. Tilly's best stocking present was the tiny dollhouse to go in *her* dollhouse, the one she had seen and loved in the shop back in November. And her favorite *proper* present from Mom and Dad was a wooden box with real pastels and watercolor paints and brushes, and a real artist's notebook with thick cream paper. That, and a new dress and leggings. She had put them on right away. Dad had cooked a Christmas lunch, and Tilly had eaten most of what was on her plate. In a minute, they would watch a movie together. Tilly wished this day would go on and on forever.

"Open the door, please, Tilly," Dad called out.

Tilly went over to let him in. He was carrying a tray with tea and cake and a bowl of clementines. He set the tray down on the coffee table and went to put another log on the fire.

"Time for your movie," Dad said. "Switch on the TV."

"What about Mom?" Tilly said.

"What about me?" Mom said.

81

"I thought you were asleep!"

"Only a little nap," Mom said. "I want to see the movie with you. I used to love this one. I first saw it when I was your age. With my sisters."

"Would you like a sister?" Dad asked Tilly. "Or a brother?"

"I don't know," Tilly said. "I've never had one."

Mom laughed. "Not long now, though. February. Less than two months, Tilly!"

The music was starting for the film. The title came up: *The Railway Children*. Tilly settled down to watch, leaning back against the sofa close to Mom. Dad poured the tea.

"Turn off the light," Mom said. "Let's watch it by the light from the candles and the fire and the lights on the tree."

Outside it was dark. Inside, it was warm and safe and everything was going to be all right.

Chapter 14

Tilly woke with a start. It was pitch dark, the middle of the night. She lay still, listening out for whatever it was that had woken her. With a horrible rush she remembered tomorrow was Monday, the first day back at school after the holidays.

A thin strip of light shone under the bedroom door; someone must have switched on the hallway light. She heard footsteps running downstairs, and not long after, the sound of a car and the slam of a car door, and the click of the front door being opened and then closed again. Low voices: Dad and another voice she didn't recognize.

Tilly's chest ached. Something bad had happened to Mom. She knew it, deep inside. Dad had called the doctor…

She listened more. Dad and the doctor came up the

stairs, went along the hallway. A door clicked shut again and she couldn't hear anything for a long time. Tilly's head was hot. Her hands made fists under the covers. She wished Little Fox was there to hold on to. She knew what Little Fox would say: she had to lie very still and very quiet. She shouldn't open the door. She must concentrate on keeping Mom safe by thinking about her. If she concentrated really hard, Mom would be all right.

Tilly imagined Mom surrounded with blue, healing light. The blue light was like a halo around Mom, keeping her safe and making her better. She must keep the blue light steady in her mind, with no gaps.

What was that?

A cry, a bit like the fox, only it was Mom crying out, as if she was hurt.

Tears pushed out from under Tilly's eyelids and she couldn't stop them. Hot, strong tears that made her eyes sting.

There were more footsteps: someone padding out to the bathroom and back. Tilly's ears hurt with so much listening, straining. Running water, more footsteps, doors opening and closing, hushed voices.

Tilly held on to the edge of the blanket; she was cold,

so cold, right to her toes. She pulled the blanket up higher, right up to her ears, and then over them, so she couldn't hear anything more.

And then she must have fallen asleep, and so she'd stopped thinking about Mom in the blue light and…

Tilly woke up again, and this time it was daylight.

Dad was standing in the doorway, running his hand through his dark hair, and smiling. "Up you go, Tilly. We've all overslept this morning!"

The events in the night came back to Tilly in a sudden, anxious rush.

"Mom?" she whispered. "Is she—what happened?" But even as she spoke the words she was wondering, had she been dreaming again? Because everything seemed to be all right now that Dad was there, smiling as if everything was normal.

Dad came over and drew the curtains back. Outside, a thick, white mist swirled around the house. "Such a heavy frost!" Dad said. "We should put some food out for the birds. Everything's frozen hard."

Dad sat down on the end of Tilly's bed. "We had a bit of a busy night, Tilly. Mom wasn't well, and the doctor came, but Mom's going to be fine. You shouldn't worry."

Tilly wanted to pull the covers over her head again.

But Dad was pushing them back, stroking her hair. "I'm going to take her in to the hospital later today. Then the doctors will be right on hand to help if we need them, and that will help Mom relax." He kept smoothing her hair. "So, Granny is going to come and stay for a few days to look after you. She can take you to school and cook your tea and things like that."

"I don't want to go to school," Tilly whispered. "I want to stay here."

The phone started ringing downstairs.

Dad stood up. "Please don't make this any harder, Tilly. Just get dressed and ready for school. That's my girl." He was already out the door and running to pick up the phone.

Tilly didn't put on her school clothes. She slipped on her dressing gown instead and padded down the landing to see Mom. She knelt on the rug by the bed and rested her head on the covers.

Mom reached out a pale hand and stroked Tilly's head. "Hello, lambkin," she said.

Tilly swallowed hard. "I feel sick," she whispered. "And my throat hurts."

"Poor you," Mom said. "You'd better get back to bed. And get an old bowl from the cupboard under the sink, in case you actually are sick. You look feverish."

Tilly stayed there a bit longer. She did feel sick, really she did. And cold and then hot.

Dad came in with a cup of tea for Mom. "That was the doctor on the phone, again," he told her. "She wants me to take you up to the hospital this afternoon."

Mom nodded. "Poor Tilly's not feeling well, either," she said. "I think she should stay home today."

Dad sighed.

"Can I get into your bed, with you?" Tilly asked Mom.

"Just for a very short time," Mom said.

It was warm, snuggled next to Mom in the big bed. Tilly wished she could stay there all day, close up and safe. But Mom had to lie on her side, and after a while, she said she was too hot with Tilly pressed up so close, so Tilly got out again and wandered back to her own room.

Dad brought up a bowl and put it by the bed. "Rest there," he said. "I'm going to do some work in the study, but you can call me if you need me. I'll leave the door open."

Now that she knew she didn't have to go to school, Tilly didn't feel quite so sick. She got up and pulled on her jeans, her thick wool sweater, and pink socks. She stood at the window; the mist was lifting and a pale sun was shining onto the icy garden, turning the frost into a million trillion sparkly jewels along every leaf and branch and blade of grass.

The house seemed different in the daytime on a school day. It was very quiet and still. But through the window she saw the tree full of tiny birds, hopping from branch to branch. Tilly padded downstairs to the kitchen and took a big chunk of bread from the bread box. She opened the fridge and found a lump of cheese and some leftover potatoes in a bowl. She put on her coat and boots and went out into the garden, closing the door very quietly behind her.

A flock of brown birds flew up from the grass into the

tree and watched while she shredded up the bread and cheese and scattered it on the ground. One brave bird flew back down and started to peck at the crumbs, and soon the others did the same. They were all so hungry. The longer she stayed, the braver they got. The usual robin flew over from the hedge and sat on the arm of the bench, right up close, watching her with its beady eye. She held out a piece of cheese and the robin hopped closer, not quite taking it from her hand at first. It took three tries, Tilly sitting as still as she could, and then at last it hopped up and took the cheese crumb out of her cupped hand. Its beak tickled and she giggled, and the robin flew up into the tree.

The fox must be hungry too. Tilly ran over the grass, through the gate into the other garden.

She saw him right away, sitting up with his scrawny tail wrapped over his paws. It was as if he had been waiting for her, had known she would come. Almost as if he were a tame fox. His ears pricked up, and he watched her intently but he didn't run off. Tilly crept toward him, holding out a piece of cold potato. His nose twitched. He stood up, wary, and she threw the food onto the frosty grass. He darted forward, picked it up in his mouth, and ran back toward the brambles. He gulped it down and then looked back at Tilly. She held out another chunk. But he was too scared of her still. He edged forward and then stopped, nose twitching, his eyes fixed on her. So she threw him the potato and the cheese, and he dashed forward and gobbled them down, and still he wanted more.

"Wait there for me!" Tilly said. She ran back to the kitchen, to find more food he might like. Meat would be good, but there wasn't any in the fridge. A raw egg? Vegetables?

"Tilly! Are you feeling better?" Dad came into the kitchen and filled the kettle from the tap. "Should I make you some breakfast? Scrambled eggs and buttered toast?"

"Yes, please," Tilly said, thinking of the hungry fox.

While Dad made her eggs and toast he talked about Granny. "Soon as she's here I can drive Mom up to the hospital. I'll come home once Mom's settled in."

"How long does she have to be there?" Tilly asked. "Why can't she stay here? I can look after her if you let me stay at home too."

"Hey, Tilly! It's safest for Mom there, like I explained before. Yes? And it will just be a week or so probably. Granny's looking forward to seeing you. You can visit Mom every day. The time will whizz by." Dad spooned the eggs onto brown toast and put the plate on the table. "There you go."

Tilly took the butter down from the shelf. But she wasn't hungry. Not one bit. She waited while Dad made

his tea and took it back to his study, and then she took the plate outside with her, for the fox.

Tilly heard Granny's car. She ran to open the front door ready for her.

"Tilly!" Granny gave her a big hug.

Granny smelled delicious: lemony and herby, like a summer garden. Held close up to her soft sweater, Tilly felt safe for a moment. But it was hard to be happy for long. Already Dad was getting the car ready to take Mom away, making it comfortable for her with a blanket and cushions. He put Mom's bag in the trunk, and it looked too big and full of stuff, Tilly thought, as if Mom was going away for a long time and not just a few days.

"See you very soon," Mom said brightly, though her face was pale and blotchy. "Don't worry, Tilly."

Tilly closed her eyes tight while the car went down the road. She imagined the blue light around Mom, like a soft blanket, tucking her in and making her better.

Tilly showed Granny around the house. This was the first time she'd visited them since they'd moved in the autumn. Granny got the vacuum out from the closet under the stairs, and then the broom and dustpan for the kitchen, and more cloths and cleaning things for the bathroom. "We'll give each room a good going over," she said.

Tilly helped. Granny sang and talked and Tilly felt much better. When they got to Dad's study, Granny opened the door and made a funny humming noise, and then she shut it again. "We'll leave that one be," she said.

"Well! It's certainly roomy, your new house!" Granny said when finally they sat down for some tea. "All those high ceilings: no wonder it's cold. It needs a thorough airing: sunshine and fresh air. If it's sunny tomorrow morning, that's what we'll do: open all the windows and give it a freshen-up!"

Granny had brought a cake: lime with coconut icing. Tilly licked the fine shreds of lime peel from the top. They made her tongue fizz.

"Now eat some actual cake!" Granny said. "You're much too thin and pale, Tilly."

Tilly ate as much as she could, very slowly. She told Granny about the hungry birds.

JULIA·GREEN

"You can show me the garden tomorrow," Granny said. "When it's light."

The day had gone so fast. Much faster than a normal school day. Tilly and Granny went around the house together, closing the curtains. Granny turned the radiators on high. She switched on all the lights. "I know it's a bit extravagant," she said, "and not good for the planet, but just tonight, we need to get rid of all those shadows." In the living room, she made a fire with logs, and then she lit candles and lined them up along the shelf. It looked like Christmas all over again.

Granny cooked macaroni and cheese for supper. Tilly was hungry for the first time in weeks. At bedtime, Granny ran the bath for Tilly, and afterward, she sat on Tilly's bed and read her a story. Tilly snuggled under the blanket to listen. Granny's voice made her feel sleepy.

"Will Dad be home soon?" Tilly asked.

"Very soon," Granny said. "Don't you worry about a thing, Tilly darling. Now it's time for sleep. Where's that old cuddly fox you used to like?"

"He's disappeared," Tilly said. "I can't find him anywhere."

94

"Hmmm. Well, you will have to put up with me instead!" Granny laughed, and leaned forward to cuddle Tilly.

Tilly was sooo sleepy. She closed her eyes.

"What you need is a cat," Granny said. "Or perhaps a dog."

"I'd like a fox," Tilly said, half asleep.

"You can't keep a fox as a pet," Granny said. "A fox is a wild animal."

"I've got one already…" Tilly whispered, already dreaming.

Chapter 15

It was the dead of night. Tilly crept out of her bed, lifted her bathrobe from the hook on the back of the bedroom door, and wrapped it around her snugly. She slid her feet into her soft slippers and opened the door. Along the landing she went, quiet as a ghost; down the stairs, across the hall into the dark kitchen. Tilly didn't stop to put on her coat or boots, although she did pick up a slice of cake from the plate on the table and put it in her pocket.

She slid back the big bolt at the bottom of the back door and turned the heavy key in the lock. She stepped down onto the path and tiptoed around the side of the house to the lawn.

Above her, the sky was crystal clear, lit by a hundred

million stars and a silver moon. The air was brittle with cold, and every blade of grass and every leaf and twig and petal and bud glittered with frost. Tilly's breath made smoke clouds. Her toes curled into her slippers, so cold and hard was the ground. She pulled up the fleecy hood of the robe and tugged the belt closer around her middle.

Her fingers almost stuck to the ice-cold metal of the garden gate when she opened it to go through. She warmed them with her mouth. She shivered and shook, but still she kept going, across the path and through the wooden gate, into her enchanted garden, through the high grass to her den. The moon and stars fizzled and glittered, loud enough for her to hear, like electricity humming along a wire. In the silver light, the frosted clumps of grass and plants and seed heads stood stiff and tall like sculptures. Her blood tingled along her veins, her heart pumped, as if it was scared it too would freeze stiff and still. It was beautiful and dangerous tonight in the magic garden.

Amber eyes gleamed from deep in the thicket of brambles. Fox eyes, Tilly told herself, and nothing to be frightened of. She fished into her pocket for the cake, crouched down near the place where the tunnel began,

and held it out. She sensed rather than saw the fox lean forward, its nose twitching. It edged forward, little by little. The fox looked as if it too had been turned to frost: every hair on its coat gleamed silver. Not a white Arctic fox, but her own magical silver fox.

Her hand shook, holding out the cake. Now the fox was so close, she could smell him. His strange, strong, animal scent. Delicately, he stretched out his head, and carefully, so he didn't hurt her, he took the cake from her hand and gulped it down. This time, he didn't run off to hide in his den in the bramble thicket. He sat down. He looked at her with his golden eyes.

Tilly, as delicate as the fox, stretched out her hand and touched the fur on his head. He felt cold and surprisingly soft. She stroked the place between his ears, and the fox let her. And then he stood up and turned and walked away into the garden.

Tilly followed after the fox. The garden was secret and dark, full of the sounds of the night. Rustlings and stirrings in the thicket under the brambles. The flapping wings of a bird. Farther off, a car engine, and high up and invisible, an airplane traveling across continents. In the cold air, sounds seemed to carry more easily.

The fox went steadily through the frozen grass and Tilly went after it, brushing against the iced branches of the shrubs and overgrown bushes on either side. When Tilly's robe got caught on a thorn, the fox waited while she unhooked it, then padded onward. All the time, its ears and tail twitched, sensitive to sounds too tiny for Tilly to hear.

The garden seemed vast, a wilderness. They crossed through the wood, darker than ever, and out the other side to a lawn Tilly had never seen before, and a frozen pond with a statue of a girl, laced with frost. There were other statues, dotted around the edge of the lawn: a stone hare, nose pointing to the moon, and a stone dove. Ahead of them now, Tilly saw the deeper shadow of a house. As they got nearer, she saw it more clearly, lit by moonlight: a tiled roof, two chimneys at each end; white walls; green-painted bay windows; and a green front door.

Tilly heard a voice singing. The girl's voice, high and clear. It was the same tune she'd heard that very first time but much louder. This time she could hear the words. The song was about a dress with green sleeves...

The fox stopped.

Tilly stopped too.

The voice seemed to be coming from one of the evergreen trees close to the house. Tilly peered up. There was a dark shadow among the other shadows, something moving…swinging back and forth. A leg, ending in a buttoned-up boot.

The singing stopped.

The girl jumped down from the tree.

She smiled. "Hello, Tilly!"

"What were you doing up in the tree?" Tilly asked.

"It's my tree house. See? Like a nest, up in the yew tree with the birds."

Tilly stood right underneath the tree and peered up. Now she could see there was a small wooden platform, built onto the thick branches at the center of the old tree. "How lovely!" Tilly said.

"You can go up and see if you like. You have to climb up." The girl looked down at Tilly's feet in muddy slippers and frowned. "Maybe another time." She smiled at Tilly. "Aren't you cold, dressed like that?"

And suddenly Tilly was, though she hadn't felt it before.

The fox barked.

The girl laughed and ran over to the fox. She took something out of her pocket and held it out. The fox took the food delicately in its teeth and swallowed it down. The girl ran her hand along his frost-silvered fur, right to the tip of his tail, and he let her. He sat down, scratched himself, and yawned.

Tilly shivered.

The girl peered at Tilly. "You look half-frozen!" she said. "I'd ask you in, except it is so very late, and I'm not supposed to be playing outside. Only it's so beautiful, with the frost and the moonlight, I couldn't resist…"

"What's your name?" Tilly whispered, but the girl turned away just at that moment. A light had gone on inside the house.

The front door opened, an oblong of light. A woman stood on the front step, looking out into the garden, and behind her, Tilly glimpsed a hallway with rose-patterned wallpaper and a tiled floor.

Tilly stepped back into the shadows. The fox did too.

"Helen? What are you doing out there?" The woman's voice was loud enough for Tilly to hear every word.

The girl turned back for a moment. "Wait here," she whispered to Tilly. "I'll come out again if I can…"

Tilly watched the girl go into the house. Framed in the doorway, in the light, she could see her red-brown hair, her green woollen coat, and her brown boots, same as before. Same as...what? Tilly couldn't think what; she just knew they were familiar somehow.

The garden seemed darker now the door had shut out the light from the house. It was colder than ever. She shouldn't be here.

Tilly thought guiltily about Granny; she imagined her waking up, coming to see if everything was all right, finding Tilly's bed empty and the back door unlocked... But the girl—Helen—had said "wait."

She waited. The door stayed shut. There was no sign of Helen.

Tilly wondered what time it was. She was shivering with cold. Tired. Now, all she wanted was to be back at home, warm and safe in bed.

The fox was sniffing at a pile of dead leaves at the edge of the lawn.

"Take me back," Tilly whispered.

As if it understood completely, the fox started picking its way back across the silvery grass, past the stone statues and the pond, toward the darker line of trees. Tilly followed. It seemed to take forever. The fox made its way steadily through the trees, twisting and turning along paths that were invisible to Tilly, dipping and ducking under fallen branches that Tilly had to climb over. She was afraid the fox would leave her behind, but each time it waited patiently for her to catch up. She was exhausted and frozen, and still they had farther to go, until at last they were out the other side of the woods. She could see the wooden fence, and the rickety gate, and she was nearly home.

Far away, an ambulance siren echoed in the frozen night.

Chapter 16

Tilly woke up, late, to a different sound: music. Granny was singing along to the radio. By the time she'd got dressed and gone downstairs, Granny had already flung open all the windows to let in the fresh air. Light flooded the house, but it was so cold!

"You'll need at least two extra thick sweaters on today, Tilly!" Granny said. "Inside and out!"

The house already seemed different with Granny sorting things out. The washing machine was whirring in the kitchen, and sheets and blanket covers were hung out on a line across the lawn.

Tilly looked at the clock. It was half past nine already! She'd forgotten all about school and so had Granny. Neither of them mentioned it. It was as if they both agreed that there was something more important to be done today. The horrible feeling in her stomach she got when it was a school day began to ebb away.

"Your dad's already gone back to the hospital. He sent his love. Your mom's doing fine. We'll go and see her later," Granny said.

After breakfast, Granny put on her coat. "Right. Now you can show me the garden."

Tilly took the crusts from her toast with them. She showed Granny how the birds flew down from the tree to be fed. The robin perched on the bench again. Granny followed behind while Tilly took the route down the path next to the raspberry bushes, down to the apple trees and along past the prickly bushes (*gooseberries*, Granny said) to the clump of funny nobbly pink stumps (*rhubarb*) and the hedge with leaves on it (*beech*). Granny kept stopping to look closer at dried up bits of plants.

"Look, Tilly!" Granny was smoothing away dead leaves to show her something hidden underneath.

Tilly saw tiny pink flowers with petals like folded-back ears, and gray-green heart-shaped leaves.

"They're called cyclamen," Granny said.

Granny showed her the tiny, pale green tips of snowdrops already poking up through the earth, ready for spring. "It looks like everything's dead in the winter garden, but it's all just there, waiting under the earth, already alive and growing."

They found a twiggy tree with pink sweet-scented flowers growing out of the tips of the bare branches. Granny broke off some twigs to take inside. "Viburnum: that'll look nice on the kitchen table." She picked some ivy to go with it.

They had reached the two bushes on either side of the gate. Granny stopped and looked through the gate to the grassy path. "Where does that go?" she asked Tilly.

"I don't know."

"We should go and explore later."

"There's a fox," Tilly said quietly. "It comes into the garden at night."

Granny looked at Tilly. "How exciting!" she said. "Perhaps it comes along that path. Now, I need to put in the next load of washing. Do you want to come back with me or stay and play in the garden?"

"Back with you."

Granny made hot berry drink for Tilly and herself. "I phoned the school earlier," she said to Tilly. "I said you're still a little under the weather."

"Am I?"

"Not exactly. But I know it's hard for you, Tilly, with your mom being ill…"

Tilly didn't want to talk about it. But it was a huge relief that she didn't have to go to school.

"We'll bring her some flowers later," Granny said. "Why don't you go and pick some more viburnum sprigs? She'll love that. They'll smell sweet as anything."

Tilly took the kitchen scissors from the silverware drawer and went into the garden again. She'd pick a huge bunch of the flowering twigs, the ones where the flowers were fully open and smelled the sweetest.

Tilly stepped back inside the kitchen and laid the bunch of twigs on the table. Granny was talking to someone out in the hallway.

Tilly listened. She couldn't help it.

"It's a real sign of anxiety, sleepwalking," Granny was

saying. "I know, it's understandable. But anything could have happened…Yes, I know."

Who was *sleepwalking*? Was she talking about Mom? Tilly wondered.

Granny came back into the kitchen. She smiled at Tilly and pointed to the phone she was holding.

"We'll see you in about an hour, then," Granny said into the phone. "Lovely. Bye for now." Granny turned to Tilly. "Your dad. Everything's fine. I told him we'll be at the hospital right after lunch."

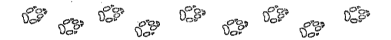

Tilly didn't like the look of the hospital. She didn't like the smell, either. She was glad she'd brought the flowers from the garden for Mom.

They found her in a room by herself, not with the other women in the ward. The big window had a view of the hills and the tops of trees, and down over the parking lot if you stood close and looked down.

"They smell gorgeous!" Mom said when Tilly brought the flowers up close. "And how are you, lambkin?"

"I'm not a lambkin," Tilly said crossly.

Dad went to get coffee.

Tilly tried out the headphones for the TV and the radio, and next she fidgeted with the things on Mom's night-stand, and then there wasn't anything to do. Granny and Mom were whispering softly together. She picked up the chart on the end of Mom's bed, which had lines, and red crosses and scribbles in messy writing. She wished Little Fox were here. She went off to explore by herself anyway.

No one took much notice of her. She walked past a ward full of women all laughing and joking, and one of them waved at her. Then she went through some swing-ing doors and along a corridor and through another door labeled *Special Neonatal Unit.*

Through a long glass window on one side of the corridor, she saw a small room full of plastic cribs and loads of tubes and wires and things, and the tiniest real babies she had ever seen, with funny knitted bonnets and mittens. Some were lying on sheepskin, and they all had tubes taped to their tiny noses. Tilly couldn't stop herself from staring until a nurse suddenly saw her and whisked a curtain back across the window.

That squirmy-eel feeling was in her stomach sud-denly. She was hot all over. She started running back to find Mom, scared she might have forgotten the way, but phew! There it was: the swinging door with its blue sign: Prenatal Ward. She leaned against the heavy door, her heart thumping too hard in her chest. She closed her eyes; she could feel it, *thump thump*, the blood rushing in her ears. Those tiny babies, all covered in wires and tubes, lying all alone in the plastic cribs; it had looked all wrong and terrible.

Tilly went more slowly along the corridor and pushed open the door to Mom's room. Granny and Dad were sipping coffee from plastic cups, and Mom was smiling. Tilly let out a long breath. She sat on the bottom of Mom's bed and watched a pigeon preening its feathers on the windowsill while the grown-ups talked.

"So what did the doctor say?" Granny asked Mom. "How long does she think it will be?"

"Soon, now. If not, they'll do a caesarean."

"Have you got everything ready? Do you need me to buy you anything?"

"We've got most of the stuff already, from when we had Tilly," Dad said.

The pigeon tapped the window with its beak. It bent its head and looked at Tilly with its beady eye.

Tilly stood up. The pigeon flew off. She watched it fly down onto the parking lot and start pecking at half a sandwich lying in the gutter. She thought about the hungry fox and about the girl living in that old house. The girl called *Helen*.

"Can we go now?" Tilly asked Granny.

"Whenever you like," Granny said.

"Thanks for coming," Mom said. "It was wonderful to see you, Tilly. Your pretty twigs have filled the whole room with their sweet scent."

Tilly leaned over to kiss Mom good-bye. She walked away as quickly as she could, before the tears came.

Granny drove fast. When they stopped at a red traffic light, she reached across for Tilly's hand.

Tilly pulled her hand away.

"Has Dad explained Mom's illness to you, Tilly? I mean properly, so you understand?"

Tilly bit down on her lip. She didn't answer.

"As soon as the baby comes, Mom will get better," Granny said. "For now, because of her headaches and high blood pressure, she has to lie down and rest and be extra careful."

Tilly watched a cyclist go past the car, to the front

of the traffic line. He had a little seat on the back, for a child. She tried to block out Granny's voice. She didn't want to think about the words.

Granny was saying something about *your baby brother or sister.*

A picture came into Tilly's head of those tiny babies in the incubator, struggling to breathe and eat, born too soon. And then the lights went green and they were off again, and Granny was quiet, concentrating on driving them home.

Granny cooked sausages and baked potatoes for supper, but Tilly wasn't hungry.

"Can I go out to play in the garden?" she asked.

"It's dark, Tilly! And too cold. Wait until the morning."

Tilly knew the fox would be hungry. When the telephone rang and Granny went to answer it, she picked up her leftover lunch and wrapped it in kitchen paper. She slipped out of the back door and ran fast across the damp grass to the garden gate. "Fox?" she called.

She waited, but no fox appeared. Anxious now, she

pushed the potato and sausage through the gate onto the grass path and ran back to the kitchen before Granny realized she'd gone out.

It was bedtime. Dad was still at the hospital.

"I don't need you to read me a story," Tilly told Granny. "I'm too sleepy tonight."

"Well," Granny said, "in that case, I'll run myself a bath and have an early night too. It's been a busy day. I hope you sleep better."

What was Granny talking about?

Tilly tried hard to stay awake. She listened to Granny pottering about, having her bath and sorting her things out in the spare room at the end of the landing. She watched the shadows dance around the room, from the lamp by her bed. She propped herself up on the pillows so she could see the dollhouse better. Was Helen in bed yet? Or still up, climbing trees, or running around the garden? Perhaps she was sitting in the den or playing with the fox…the fox she'd somehow tamed.

Tilly climbed out of bed again and drew back the

curtains, to look out. All she could see was her own reflection. She turned off the bedside light and looked again, her face pressed against the cold glass. The dark shapes of trees and bushes were swaying in the wind, and clouds moved fast across the moon. The first spatter of rain hit the window. Tilly climbed back into bed. She listened to the rain and the wind battering the house. The fox would be safe and dry in its den, deep in the bramble thicket. She hoped it had found the food she left earlier.

She still hadn't heard Dad come back home from the hospital. The knot of worry inside her was getting bigger, taking up all the space.

Chapter 17

Well, you did sleep well!" Granny whisked back the curtains in Tilly's room. "Right through that storm and everything!"

Daylight flooded the room. As Tilly woke up, the pain in her stomach came back too. "Is Dad here?" she said.

"He stayed the night with Mom, at the hospital," Granny said in her extra cheerful voice. "I expect he thought it would be lonely for your mom, all by herself."

Tilly reached out a hand for the little clock on her bedside table. "Twenty to ten!" she said.

"Yes! It's much too late for you to go to school now. So we'll have another day doing nice things together."

"Won't school be upset?"

"No. I've explained everything to your teacher. If you feel up to it, you can write some more of your story, she says."

Tilly didn't ask what exactly Granny had *explained.* The relief at not having to go to school flooded over her.

Granny was still talking. "So, get washed and dressed and then you can go and see if the storm did any damage in the garden. And we have to feed those birds."

Tilly tried to eat the bowl of porridge, since Granny had made it specially, with brown sugar melting on the top. She managed two spoonfuls, and then she put on her coat and boots, and ran outside before Granny could say anything.

The birds were waiting for her in the tree. They flew down for toast crumbs, no longer scared of her, and a robin chirped from the bench and followed her as she went through the gate and across into the wild garden. The food she'd left out for the fox was gone.

A large branch had fallen in the storm. Tilly had to climb over it. The bark was wet and slippery and stained her hands green. Everything was sopping wet. The long grass had been flattened and the old rose had fallen off the wall.

Tilly went farther across the wild garden.

She gasped. Her den had partly collapsed; the branches had fallen down; the woven grass was just a soggy mess.

She stared at it and then she set to work, tugging the branches back into position, mending it as best she could.

She wished Helen would come and help her. She looked around, in case she was watching, hidden in a tree or playing in another part of the garden, but the garden just seemed empty. There was no one here. No sound of singing or rustling of leaves. Even the birds seemed quiet. Drips rained down from the trees overhead every time the wind blew the wet branches.

Tilly started putting back the spiral of pebbles, arranging the scattered stones in size order. Her hands were freezing cold, and the pebbles felt clammy and horrid. She put the log table back upright in the middle of the den, and then she saw something else, half hidden under a pile of dead bracken: the corner of an old square tin box. She pulled it out, pried open the lid.

Inside she found a stump of candle and a book.

Tilly took out the book very carefully. It was old, like the ones in Dad's study, with a green cover and thick cream pages and pictures. Black and white line drawings on almost every page, and just a few in color, on a page by themselves, with a sheet of very thin, almost transparent paper over the top, which you had to lift up so you could see the pictures. Carefully, she turned the pages.

The edges of the pages were mottled with brown spots, as if the book had gotten wet. Helen must have left it here, before the storm in the night. Tilly imagined her reading the book by the light of the candle, snug in Tilly's den.

Tilly half expected to hear her at any moment, singing that tune that seemed to get right into her head. But there was only the drip, drip of water running off the leaves and branches in the trees

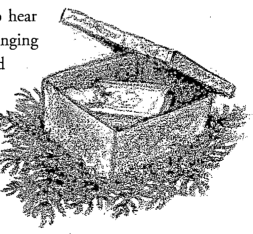

and shrubs around her, and the call of some bird, repeating the same two notes over and over.

There was no sign of the fox. Tilly could see where the grass and brambles had been squashed down as it made its way to its den each day. In the soft mud at the edge, she thought she could make out paw prints. The fox was probably curled up asleep, warm and dry in the den it had hollowed out in the earth.

Well, she could try to find the house herself. Helen might be there, even though it was the morning, and a school day.

Tilly pushed her way through the thicket of trees, stumbling over fallen branches and twigs and long trailing creeper vines that dangled from the tops of the trees like ropes for monkey swings. She went past huge ferns like tongues. In the dark, she hadn't seen any of this. It was even harder work than before, clambering through the tangled wood; there wasn't a path, just a whole maze of animal tracks, and it was impossible to remember which way the fox had taken her before.

Any minute now, Tilly thought, and I'll get to the other side and the lawn with the statues and the pond and the house.

She tried for a long time, pushing through the undergrowth, getting scratched and wet, and still she couldn't find the way.

She seemed to have been gone for hours. Finally she gave up and went back home. She was nearly there. That bird was calling, repeating its cry, and then another sound echoed, like a bird, but not quite right. Like, Tilly suddenly thought, a person imitating a bird. Was Helen there, up in the tree, teasing her?

But she couldn't start searching for her now. Granny was standing at the open garden gate, looking up and down the grass path. She whirled around as she caught sight of Tilly. "Where have you been? I was really worried! Didn't you hear me calling you?"

Tilly put her arms around Granny. "Sorry," she whispered.

"You're soaking wet! What have you been doing?"

"Exploring," Tilly whispered. "Mending my den."

"You must tell me when you go off, Tilly. I'm looking after you, remember. You can't just go wandering into some old wasteland to play. It isn't safe!"

"It's a garden, not a wasteland!" Tilly said indignantly. "And it's totally safe!" And then, before she'd thought about what she was saying, "It belongs to my friend."

Granny looked at her. "And which friend is that?"

"She's called Helen."

"Hmmm," Granny said, as if she didn't believe a word of it.

Back in the warm kitchen, Granny wanted to hear more about Tilly's friend.

"What did you say her name was?"

"Helen."

Granny's eyes went narrow.

"Does she go to your school?"

Tilly shook her head. "I've only seen her twice," she said. "She lives in the house on the other side of the trees. The garden's huge."

"Well, that's nice. Should we invite her over to play here?"

Tilly didn't know what to say. But Granny was persistent.

"I've only been there through the woods, in the magic garden," Tilly said. "But there might be another way."

Granny was quiet for a bit. "Is she a real friend or a made-up one?" she finally asked.

Tilly wouldn't answer any more questions after that.

Granny made coffee for herself. Tilly frothed up the milk for her with Dad's electric whisk.

"There must be another way around to the house," Granny said. "We'll go later, you and me. We'll go for a walk, and call on Helen and invite her to tea!"

Granny put on her coat and boots.

Tilly got ready too, but slowly. She didn't want Granny interfering with her and Helen. She thought quickly what to do. Perhaps if she distracted Granny, she'd forget about finding where Helen lived.

"Let's explore where the grassy path goes, Granny," she said. "I've never been up there."

Tilly led the way, out of the garden gate, and then turned right, along the path. It ran between the two gardens, so that the tumbled-down stone wall of the magic garden was on one side and the beech hedge of Tilly's garden was on the other.

"No wonder there are foxes!" Granny said, following Tilly along the footpath. "Isn't it lovely? Like living in the countryside. You wouldn't expect it so close to the city."

The path got muddier. There were ruts and puddles.

They reached the end of both gardens; now there was an overgrown hedge on both sides and then woodland, and finally they came to a big wooden farm gate.

"Farmland," Granny said. "But there's a stile, look. So the path goes on, across the field."

Tilly climbed over the stile and then she stopped. Three horses in the field had stopped grazing and turned their heads to watch. They began to trot toward the gate. Tilly climbed quickly back over the stile.

"They only want to say hello!" Granny said.

But the horses looked huge close up. They rolled their eyes. When Granny reached her hand up to stroke their noses, they stamped their feet and reared their heads, showing their teeth. "Perhaps we won't go into their field after all," Granny said.

It started to spit with rain. "Can we go back now?" Tilly said.

"Don't you want to find Helen's house?" Granny asked. "Let's just quickly explore the other way. It would be good to have someone to play with, wouldn't it?"

It was a boring walk, back the way they'd come, and then on and on. The grass track became a stony lane, and finally it joined the road.

"If we turn right here," Granny said, "and go along the road for a bit, that should bring us to a front way into Helen's house, logically speaking." She smiled at Tilly. "We can ask her mom if she minds you going into that wild bit of garden by yourself. I'd rather be sure."

Tilly dragged her feet. This wasn't right. Through the trees she glimpsed the shape of a house, set back from the road, but it looked very different now, in the daylight. Nothing like the house she'd seen before.

Granny stopped. She was reading something, a sign nailed to a post, next to the wall.

"Land for Sale. By Auction." Granny read out the words, loud enough for Tilly to hear. "They must be selling that huge wild garden," she said. "And no wonder. It's much too big for one family to look after."

Granny waited for her to catch up.

"I want to go back," Tilly said. "I don't like it here. It's all wrong. Everything's wrong." Suddenly, everything felt all muddled and horrible. She didn't want Granny there. She wanted Mom.

She started walking back the way they'd come, fast.

Granny came after her. "Wait!" she called, but Tilly started to run.

Tilly couldn't answer Granny's questions.

The *real* answers didn't make any sense.

She didn't want to tell Granny anything.

Not about hearing Helen in the garden and finding the things she left. Or about the fox taking her to the other part of the garden, and how she'd seen Helen up a tree before she went into her house with the rose-patterned wallpaper and the tiled floor...or about Christmas Eve and their midnight feast...

Tilly wished she'd never mentioned Helen in the first place. She wished she could turn back time.

Granny filled up the kettle and switched it on. She put the teapot next to the sink and a mug on the kitchen table, ready for tea.

Tilly went upstairs to her bedroom and shut the door. She knelt down in front of the dollhouse, with its tiled roof and chimneys at either end, and its green-painted wooden bay windows and cream walls. She opened the hinged front. She got everything out of all the rooms: the people and the furniture and even the tiny pictures hanging on tiny nails on the rose-patterned walls.

She put it all in a pile, and then she found an old shoe box and dumped everything in there, and shoved it to the back of her wardrobe. She pushed the dollhouse under the bed, so she didn't have to see it anymore. She lay on the bed, and she cried.

Dad was home at last.

Tilly ran down the stairs to open the front door for him. She hugged him tight.

Dad looked surprised. "Hey, Tilly! That's a nice welcome!" He hugged her back. "Mom sends you hugs and kisses," Dad said.

They went into the kitchen to make tea for Dad. They went past the open living room door; Granny was sitting on the sofa, knitting something with fine white wool. The needles click-clicked.

Tilly looked away quickly.

"Tomorrow, I want to go to school," Tilly told Dad. "I've decided."

"Good plan," Dad said. He looked pleased. "Written any more of your story?"

Tilly shook her head.

"Me neither. How about we both work on our stories till supper time?"

While Dad tap-tapped on the laptop in his study, Tilly lay on the carpet and drew with her new pastels and watercolor paints onto thick white paper.

"My story has changed," she told Dad. "It's not about a cat anymore. It's about a fox, and a girl, and a magic garden."

"Excellent," Dad said. "The best stories change a lot while you're writing them. Can I read it when it's ready?"

Tilly nodded.

"How long do you think? Hours or days?" Dad asked.

"A day, at least!" Tilly said. "How about yours?"

"You wouldn't want to read mine!" Dad laughed. "And mine won't be ready for a long time."

"Hours or days?" Tilly asked.

"Months! A year, even!"

"What's yours about?"

Dad looked puzzled. "Well...it's about a boy growing up. And about a family, I suppose."

"It sounds boring!" Tilly said, which made Dad laugh.

It's nice, both of us working like this, Tilly thought, as she painted the fox's tail russet brown. The clock ticked. The faint sound of music on the radio drifted up the stairs. Outside, it was raining hard.

"I'm going back to see Mom after supper," Dad told Tilly. "We think the baby might be born tonight."

Chapter 18

Dad read Tilly the next chapter of her book. He looked up when he finished. "You don't really need me to read you this," he said. "I know you could read it by yourself. But I'm glad you let me read to you still." He kissed her good night. He stroked her hair.

Dad didn't seem to want to go.

"Won't Mom be needing you?" Tilly asked eventually.

Dad kissed her again. "Yes. Are *you* going to be all right?"

Tilly nodded.

"See you tomorrow, then."

Tilly's throat was tight. "Night night! Give Mom a hug from me."

She listened to Dad's feet going along the landing

and down the stairs, and then the sound of the door opening and closing, and the car engine. She imagined him arriving at the hospital; all the windows would be lit up, shining out into the dark. He would go up the stairs two at a time and walk fast along the maze of corridors, and through the swinging doors to Mom's ward, where Mom would be waiting for him.

Tilly didn't want to imagine what would happen after that. She knew a bit about babies being born. She knew it sometimes hurt a lot. And she didn't want to think about those too tiny babies who might not survive because they had been born too soon. *This* baby wasn't supposed to be born till February.

Granny tapped on the door and called out, "Goodnight, Tilly! Sweet dreams!"

"Night night, Granny," Tilly called back. But of course she wouldn't have sweet dreams. How could she, when she wouldn't be going to sleep?

She let herself doze a bit, so she would have more energy for later. She hoped Granny would go to bed early again, so she wouldn't have too long to wait.

The phone rang.

Tilly got out of bed and opened her door a little, so

she could listen to what Granny was saying, but it didn't seem to be anything important.

She shut the door again and hopped back into bed. She snuggled down under the blanket. She still had her socks on, and a sweater under her pajamas. Dad hadn't noticed. The window rattled as a gust of wind buffeted it, and she heard rain pattering onto the path outside. Inside, she was cozy. Warm as toast. Getting very sleepy...

The fox barked three times.

Chapter 19

The fox was standing at the gate. Its eyes glowed amber, watching Tilly's every movement. When Tilly held out her gifts of bacon and lime and coconut cake, the fox crept forward, its belly low, and took the food delicately from Tilly's hand without biting or hurting her. The fox gulped it down without chewing and then turned and padded toward the magic garden. Tilly watched the white tip of its tail flicker in the darkness.

Tilly picked her way through the wet grass, and climbed over the fallen tree, trying not to get the slimy green stuff on her hands. Ahead, something moved: a hand, pale, waving at her from inside the den.

"I've been here ages!" Helen said very quietly. "I hoped you'd come, and then it started raining so I wasn't sure…but I've mended the roof, look, with some old tarpaulin I found. It's quite dry inside." She shifted over to make room for Tilly.

"It's amazing!" Tilly said. "It's as good as new! Thank you!"

"Sshh!" Helen said. "Keep your voice down! We don't want to scare her off."

"Scare who?"

"The vixen. She's getting ready to have cubs, I'm sure of it now. She might even have had them. I thought I heard tiny squeaking sounds, and I stayed really quiet and still, and then the vixen came running from the trees, and she shot into the brambles."

"It's a *she* fox!" Tilly said. "I never thought of that."

Helen laughed. "She's a vixen, and this will be her first litter. And that's why she's hungry all the time. She can't find enough food for herself; it all goes on growing the babies, inside her. That's what I think, anyway."

"Is she your pet fox?" Tilly asked.

"No. You can't keep a fox as a pet. A fox is a wild animal." Helen laughed again. "But I feed her every day if I can."

"I've fed her too," Tilly said.

"I know."

Tilly's face flushed. "I waited for you that time. And I've looked and looked for you since then…but you never came. And I realized I've never seen you in the daytime. It's always the night." She looked at Helen: her smooth pale skin, her oval face framed by her red-brown hair. "But I found the book and the candle in the tin, so I knew you must have been back."

"Did you like the book?"

Tilly nodded.

"You can keep it if you like…" Helen stopped talking abruptly to listen.

Tilly listened too. "Do you think we'll see the babies?" she whispered.

"Not yet, it's too soon. And you'll have to be very careful and quiet. The fox will be extra nervous. It's very early in the spring for cubs; she'll have a hard time hunting for food."

"I gave her some cake earlier," Tilly said.

Helen sniffed. "She needs proper food."

"Like what?"

"Mice and baby rabbits and small birds and frogs. Worms, even."

Tilly shivered. "What's that?" She peered out into the dark.

Something was rustling in the undergrowth. They both leaned forward, listening.

"The trouble is," Helen whispered, "if the vixen gets disturbed she might abandon her babies. You mustn't go too close. And promise not to tell anyone they're here. Grown-ups get funny about foxes. They don't like them."

"Oh!" Tilly had a sudden, horrible thought. She remembered the words Granny had read aloud, from the sign. "What if someone buys the garden?" Tilly said. "And then they start cutting down the trees and the brambles and everything? What will happen to the fox cubs then?"

Helen looked as if she'd been stung. For a moment she sat completely still. "What do you mean, *buy the garden?*" she said. Her voice was cold and hard and quiet. "The garden belongs to us! Us and the birds and the foxes and all the wild creatures."

"There was a sign up," Tilly said. "About land for sale, and an auction or something. There was a date too."

Helen stared at her, her eyes dark in her pale face.

Tilly shivered. She felt sick. Something was terribly wrong.

Helen started scrabbling her way toward the entrance, bundling the candles and book and everything into the blanket in a terrible rush.

"Where are you going?" Tilly said. "Don't go, Helen! What's the matter? What did I say? I'm sorry...Wait!" She tried to follow Helen out through the narrow door, but it was too late. By the time she'd crawled out of the den and stood up, Helen had gone.

It was raining again: icy rain, turning to sleet.

Tilly pulled the tarpaulin over the entrance to the den, to keep it dry inside. She picked her way across the sodden garden, back toward her own house. The sleet was turning to snow; soft wet flakes of it clinging to her pajamas and her hair. Her feet were soaking wet.

137

If there's snow, there will be footprints, Tilly thought, and paw prints, and then someone will find out about the fox…And I've upset Helen and now she won't be friends with me and I'll probably never see her again…She began to cry. And now she'd started, she couldn't stop. Tears ran down her face, mixing with the wet snow, and everything was blurred, so she could hardly see the way.

"Tilly? Tilly?" Granny was saying her name and holding her arm gently, talking softly. "This way, Tilly love, everything's fine, just along here, back you go…no need to wake up." She was steering her along the mossy corridor into the bedroom, toward the white bed, like snow. Granny was rubbing her wet hair with a towel and pulling off her wet socks…

Tilly heard her own voice whispering back, saying something muddled about *babies* and *footprints,* and *Helen*…but she was so, so sleepy, drifting off, sinking back under the warm blanket, and Granny was tucking her in, smoothing her hair, soothing her back to sleep.

Chapter 20

Tilly knew she was dreaming this time, even though she was in the dream too.

She was outside, at the gate. The fox led the way, like the last time, through the wet grass and under the trees, past the fallen rose and the newly repaired den, the bramble patch, into the woods.

Tilly looked for things to remember the way: land-marks she could find in the daylight, by herself, but it was hard, in the dark, to see anything very much, and it was all the same: trees and prickly bushes and dead leaves and fallen branches; ghostly ropes of old creeper that swayed and rustled. It smelled of damp and decay and rot, musty old smells like forgotten cupboards and blocked drains.

The dark got less black as they came out of the trees, onto grass. But where before there had been a huge round lawn with stone statues, and a pond and the house with its open front door, light spilling onto the gravel path, now it was all empty and dark. The lawn was a tangle of over-grown grass and bushes; no one had cut it for years. The blank windows of the empty house looked like hollow eyes.

. She knew there was no point going forward. The house was deserted and the girl Helen was long gone.

"Take me home!" Tilly whispered.

But the fox had disappeared.

Tilly was alone in the dark, and she had no idea how to find the way back.

Granny was there again, sitting on the bed. "It's all right, Tilly," she said. "You're safe in bed, and everything's fine."

Tilly blinked, The light was glowing on the bedside table, making shadows around the room.

"You've been dreaming again," Granny said. "That's all."

Tilly looked at the clock. "Five o'clock," she said. "That's nearly morning."

"Yes. But it won't be light for another two hours, Tilly. So go back to sleep, yes? Please try."

Tilly nodded.

"Should I leave the light on?"

"Yes."

When Granny had gone back to her own room again, Tilly got out of bed to look out the window. It was snowing properly now, huge feathery flakes filling the sky, whirling down. Tilly watched it for ages.

Little by little, the horrible empty feeling from the dream drained away.

Little by little, as she sat at the window, a new feeling came. A sort of fizzing, tingling feeling, that started at the tips of her toes and went right through her, to the top of her head.

The feeling that comes when something exciting is about to happen...

Tilly watched the falling snow until her feet were too cold to bear, and then she crept back into bed and snuggled under the covers.

Outside, the garden filled softly with snow.

Chapter 21

The telephone was ringing. It seemed to fill the whole house with its urgent sound. Tilly sat bolt upright. The bedroom was full of light; she'd been asleep, and it was properly morning now. The ringing went on and on. Tilly shot out of bed and ran downstairs to pick up the phone.

"Tilly?" Dad's voice! He sounded breathless, excited. "Guess what?"

Tilly could hardly breathe. "The baby?"

"Yes! A little boy. And he's fine, and Mom's fine." Dad sounded as if he was crying.

Tilly's insides turned somersaults.

Granny was padding downstairs. She stopped at the bottom step and waited, her face full of questions.

Dad was still talking. "He's very small but completely perfect; he's breathing by himself and even feeding, and oh—you have to come and see him as soon as Granny can bring you, Tilly. Is she there? Can I speak to her?"

Tilly passed the phone to Granny.

She went into the kitchen, opened the back door, and a blast of cold air rushed in. The snow had settled on the path and the grass; not a single blade of green showed now.

She shoved her feet into her boots and ran out, leaving huge prints over the white garden. Even the tree was covered: little avalanches of snow slid off the overloaded twigs, making shooshing sounds. The snow creaked under the weight of her boots as she ran and danced and spun.

It had snowed, and her baby brother had just been born! The very same night! And now Mom would get better. Everything was going to be all right!

Tilly started picking up handfuls of snow, packing it with her bare hands, rolling it into a ball. *I'll make a snow fox, instead of a snowman! An Arctic fox.*

She remembered the book in Mrs. Almond's classroom. She swallowed hard.

But she'd decided, hadn't she? She'd told Dad she would go back to school today, and she would. There wasn't anything to be frightened of.

"Tilly?" Granny called from the back doorstep. "Come and get dressed! You'll freeze to death dressed like that!"

Tilly ran back to the kitchen.

Granny gave her a huge hug. "Isn't it the best news? Amazing and wonderful! A baby brother, Tilly!" She held Tilly tight, and Tilly squeezed her back. "We'll go and see them later," Granny said.

"Am I still going to school?" Tilly asked.

"What do you think? What would you like to do?"

Tilly took a deep breath. "School," she said. "And go and see Mom after."

"Let's get breakfast, then," Granny said.

Granny wanted to come into the classroom, but Tilly said no.

"It's not allowed," Tilly said.

"I don't see why not!" Granny huffed.

"Only the preschool classes allow moms and dads in," Tilly explained. "I'll be fine! Don't worry, Granny!"

Granny was giving her that look again, as if she didn't quite believe her.

"I'll be back at three thirty, and we'll drive straight to the hospital," Granny said. She kissed Tilly good-bye on the top of her head.

Tilly stamped her snowy boots on the mat and went down the corridor to her classroom. She hung up her wet coat and went straight in. She was early.

Mrs. Almond was sitting at her table at the front, writing notes. She looked up. "Tilly! How lovely to see you. Welcome back!"

Tilly smiled shyly.

"How's your mom?" Mrs. Almond asked.

"She's in the hospital. The baby was born last night."

"Oh, Tilly! How exciting!"

"I haven't seen them yet," Tilly said. "I'm going after school today. It's a boy."

"Has he got a name yet?"

Tilly shook her head. She went to her drawer to take out her school reading book. It seemed a long time since she'd looked at it.

"Do you want to choose something else?" Mrs. Almond said. "Have a look through the new books I've put on the shelf."

New books smell wonderful! Tilly thought. She liked being the first person to open up the pages. She chose one with a lovely cover, about an elephant. She read the first page, about a girl called Kirsty. That was Mom's name. The story made it sound as if the girl was exploring in a jungle but really she was playing. It was the sort of game Tilly liked, where you make stuff up.

The classroom was beginning to fill up. Lucy said hello to Tilly shyly, when Harriet was busy talking to Simone. A girl she didn't recognize, with lovely dark hair and eyes, came through the classroom door and hovered there, unsure. Mrs. Almond went over to the girl. She brought her over to Tilly's table. "Susila only started on Monday. Perhaps you would help her today?"

Tilly nodded.

Susila kept her eyes down, looking at the table, not at Tilly.

So Tilly had to do the talking to begin with. "I've been away for a few days," she explained. "My mom's just had a baby, and I'm going to see them this afternoon. We moved here in the middle of last term, so I've only been at this school since then."

Susila didn't speak.

Tilly tried again. "Have you just moved here too?"

Susila nodded. "From London."

"I've been to London," Tilly said. "On the train. To the Natural History Museum and the Science Museum and the London Eye."

"Which was your favorite?" Susila asked.

"I liked the Natural History Museum," Tilly said, "because of the whale and the dinosaurs, but I didn't like the stuffed animals and birds."

Susila pulled her reading book out of her bag and put it on the table.

Tilly glimpsed the title: *The Midnight Fox*. Her heart beat a little faster. She thought about her own fox, with tiny cubs, in the snow...

Mrs. Almond started to call the names for attendance.

At recess, Susila followed Tilly outside.

Harriet, Lucy, and Simone were already sitting on the bench, looking bored and cold.

Lots of other children were racing around and throwing snowballs when the teachers weren't looking. A big group from fifth grade started making an igloo.

"We could make a snow animal," Tilly said. "I was going to make a snow fox in our garden at home, but I ran out of time."

"We could make lots of little snow birds. That would be quicker," Susila said.

Two younger girls wanted to help. Other children came to watch. Soon there was a row of small snow doves on the playground. And then the bell rang and it was time to line up to go back inside.

Tilly's hands were bright red, freezing cold, but it was the first time she'd actually enjoyed recess in a long time. And after that, Tilly was just excited about going to see Mom and the baby, and it was hard to concentrate on anything else at school at all.

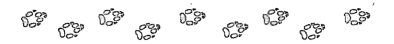

Granny was waiting for her at the gate at three thirty.

"How was it?" Granny asked.

"Good," Tilly said. "We made snow birds, but they've all melted now."

"I went shopping," Granny said, as she started the car. "I thought you might want to give a little present to the baby, and then I couldn't resist one for you. It's in that bag if you want to look."

Tilly opened the bag. Two soft animals were in there: a white polar bear and a small fox with red-brown fur and a white-tipped tail.

Granny glanced at her. "The fox is for you, to replace the one you lost."

Tilly took it out of the bag. It was quite sweet: soft, furry, all clean and new, but it was nothing like Little Fox, and anyway, you couldn't just replace one animal with another. Granny should know that!

"It's nice," she said quickly. "Thank you, Granny. But would you mind if I gave it to the baby instead?"

"As you please," Granny said. "The polar bear can be from me and the fox from you. How about that?"

"There's hardly any snow left," Tilly said sadly, as they went up the hill to the hospital. "I wish it would snow again, lots more."

Granny laughed. "Me too, but only when we're safely back at home. All of us: Mom, Dad, baby, you, and me."

"You go first," Granny said when they reached the maternity ward.

The nurse at the desk smiled at Tilly. "Who are you visiting?"

"My mom."

"Kirsty Harper," Granny said.

"Fifth door on the right."

Tilly ran ahead, counting the doors, then stopped.

She stood on tiptoe so she could look through the glass window in the door. It was like looking into a picture in a frame. Mom was in the bed but sitting up, talking to Dad, who was in the chair by the bed, one hand on the tiny mound of blanket inside a plastic crib. No wires. No horrible machines or feeding tubes.

Tilly let out her breath with a big sigh.

Slowly, she opened the door.

"Tilly!" Dad sprang up to give Tilly a huge hug. He held her so close his stubbly chin tickled her face.

Mom's eyes looked big, shiny with tears about to spill. But she looked fine too, not so pale, and now she was smiling and asking questions, and Tilly felt the huge knot of worry inside her begin to unravel.

"Here he is," Dad said, lifting the bundle out of the crib. "Get comfy next to Mom, and you can give him his first ever cuddle from his big sister."

The baby was as small as a doll, but the blanket wrapped around him made him feel more sturdy, and it wasn't so scary after all, holding him by herself. His eyes stayed tight shut, his tiny hand poking out at the top of the white blanket stayed curled in a fist. The blanket went up and down, in time with his breath.

"What should we call him?" Tilly said.

"We need to make a list," Dad said. "Any ideas, Til?"

She shook her head. Names were hard. They had to sound right and not remind you of anyone else, and they were important too, Tilly thought. They seemed to make you be the person you were. If she'd been something like Harriet or Alex, say, instead of Tilly, she'd be different...

The baby began to stir. He made tiny noises; his mouth opened a little bit, then he yawned. Tilly passed him across to Mom very, very carefully. Even though he was tiny, her arms ached.

"What do you think?" Mom said. "Will he do?"

Tilly didn't know what to say. She took the polar bear and the little fox out of the bag and perched them at the foot of the crib, so the baby could see them when he opened his eyes. "These are from Granny," she said to Mom.

"And you," Granny said.

Mom kissed her head. "Thank you, Tilly. How lovely."

Granny wanted a turn holding the baby. She said he was *beautiful*, though anyone could see he wasn't really— too scrawny and wrinkled, with skin so pale it was nearly transparent and you could see blue veins underneath.

Granny got an old envelope out of her bag. She'd scribbled her own list of names on the back. She handed it to Dad.

Dad gave Mom a funny look. "Maximilian, Benjamin, Samuel, James, Raphael, Sebastian," he read out.

Mom pulled a face.

Tilly laughed. She leaned closer into Mom's warm

body. Mom was all soft, wrapped in her fuschia-pink dressing gown. "When are you coming home?" she asked her.

"A week or so, maybe," Mom said. "They have to do tests, on me and on *him*. But then we can come home if all's well."

"And I'll be back this evening," Dad said. "We can have a special dinner to celebrate. How about that, Tilly? What should we have?"

"Pancakes, of course," Tilly said.

Chapter 22

After supper, Tilly and Dad went upstairs to find the things they'd need for when the baby came home.

"He won't have his own room to begin with," Dad explained. "He'll need to be close to Mom at night-time. New babies have to feed most of the time. But we'll have a look for the Moses basket we had for you and the blankets and your little onesies and pajamas."

"Where?" Tilly asked. "I haven't seen any of that stuff *ever*!"

"It's all in the attic," Dad said. "Packed neatly in boxes with labels, Mom says."

They had to get the ladder out. Dad let Tilly climb up first. She had to push open a hatch door in the ceiling above the landing.

"Careful where you step," Dad said. "Keep to the places where there are solid floorboards. You should find a light switch on the left, just inside the door."

The attic smelled musty and old. Tilly clambered in and stood up. For a second, before she found the light switch, she looked into the darkness and heard things rustling and shifting, scuttling. There might be spiders, or mice even.

In the light, she saw ancient cobwebs looping the roof joists and piles of cardboard boxes, stacked-up wooden furniture, a big wooden chest.

"Scoot over," Dad said from the top of the ladder. "Then I can come up too."

Dad had to duck down; the roof wasn't high enough for him to stand upright except in the middle, where the roof pointed.

Tilly found the Moses basket. It was lined with pale blue cotton cloth with a rabbit pattern. Inside, on the foam mattress, was a plastic bag full of white cotton blankets, little sheets, and something furry.

"Sheepskin!" Dad said, looking over her shoulder.

"Did I sleep in this?" Tilly asked.

"You did! Imagine that, you really were that size once." He laughed.

While Dad searched for the cardboard box contain-
ing the baby clothes, Tilly explored the attic. The boards
didn't reach as far as the edges. If she made a mistake,
she might step right through the ceiling underneath! She
tried to figure out which bit of the house was under the
different areas of the attic.

An oval table and two wooden chairs were stacked
over where her bedroom must be. "Where did these
come from?" she asked.

"More of Miss Sheldon's things," Dad said. "There
are all sorts of odds and ends of hers still up here. We'll
have to sort it all out eventually. Get rid of the things we
don't need."

Tilly opened up the lid of the wooden chest. The attic
light threw strange shadows. She needed a flashlight,
really, to see inside. She put her hand in and pulled out
the top layers of material.

"Look! Dress up clothes!" Tilly said. "A whole box
full." She pulled out more skirts and dresses, old-
fashioned things made of silky material that slithered
through her fingers. In the dim light it was hard to see
the colors properly, but there were white lacy things,
petticoats or nighties, perhaps, and a thick black

skirt that reached down to the ground when she held it against herself, and a flowery dress, a feathery scarf, a green coat with a velvet collar and a pair of soft shoes the same color, some leather ankle boots with little buttons that laced up, too big for Tilly but nice all the same. Helen would love these! Tilly thought, and then she squashed the thought down again because... Because she wasn't sure about Helen anymore.

"Right, that's everything for now," Dad said. "Shall we go down?"

Tilly hauled the clothes back into the chest and shut the lid.

She went down the ladder first and caught the basket and the piles of baby clothes and things as Dad threw them down to her. They took the clothes and bedding and put them in the washing machine to get them clean and ready.

Granny was reading in the living room, her glasses slipping down her nose. Dad poured a drink for her and himself and put another log on the fire. "Bedtime, Tilly," he said. "It's been a long day! And there's school tomorrow. Run along and get ready. You can read *one* chapter in bed, that's all."

Tilly closed the living room door behind her and stood for a second in the hall. The dark wasn't scary anymore, she realized, even with the coats and things hanging up making shadows. She knew it was late, but she had one important thing to do before she got into bed. She listened to the rise and fall of Dad's and Granny's voices, cozy and comforting behind the shut door. She went quietly into the kitchen, took three leftover cold pancakes from the fridge and two eggs, and then she put on her boots and coat and ran out into the garden.

Most of today's snow had gone. She left the food by

the garden gate like last time and called softly for the fox. She waited. Was that something moving?

Sure enough, she heard rustling and then the shadow of the fox came across from the wild garden to the other side of the footpath. Its ears were pricked up, its nose sniffing the air, the bushy tail held low, twitching. She crouched, waiting, and gradually, step by slow step, the fox came closer. Tilly held her breath. The fox's golden eyes gleamed. Its breath made clouds on the cold night air. It came right up and stopped, and picked up one of the eggs and ran back with it across the footpath to the wild garden. Tilly watched closely. She was sure this was a different fox: not nearly as scruffy and thin as the vixen. Was it the father fox, helping bring food for the cubs and the vixen?

Tilly hoped it was. It made her happier, to know the vixen was not so alone, struggling to find food and guard the cubs by herself.

She stood up. It was much too cold to stay any longer. She ran back to the kitchen and upstairs to her room.

Later, Dad came up to say good night. "I didn't think you'd still be awake," he said. "I'll wake you up at seven and take you to school tomorrow, okay? Let Granny sleep in. Sweet dreams!"

"That's what Granny always says," Tilly answered, sleepily.

"Of course. She said it to me when I was a boy," Dad said. "And that's why I say it to you."

Tilly remembered a photo at Granny's house of Dad when he was about eight. The funny thing was, you could see it was Dad even then, even with more hair and wearing shorts.

"Start thinking of some names for your brother," Dad said. He blew her a kiss from the doorway. "Something better than Granny's suggestions!"

But Tilly was already fast asleep.

Chapter 23

Dad took Tilly to school by car in the morning because he was going to go straight to the hospital as soon as he'd dropped her off.

"Emil, Jonah, Noah, Toby, Todd?" Dad said. "Like any of them?"

"Toby or Todd," Tilly said. "Then we'll both be Ts."

She flipped through the pages of the baby names book on her lap. She read out more funny ones. "How about Norbert? It means 'Bright North,' in old English."

Dad laughed.

"Or Orson, from the Latin for bear."

She looked for her own name and frowned. "Tilly isn't in this stupid book!"

Dad glanced over at her. "Try under Matilda," he said.

"*Matilda, meaning 'mighty in battle.' Short forms: Matti, Tilda, Tilly,*" she read aloud.

"See? That about sums you up, Tilly!"

"What does?"

"Mighty in battle. It means you're brave. You have courage and spirit. And so you do."

They'd got to school. Dad parked the car under the trees next to the playground. "Should I come in?"

Tilly shook her head.

"Want to invite someone to come over after school?" Dad asked.

"Maybe," Tilly said. She picked up her bag from the backseat, got out, and slammed the car door.

Dad wound down the window. "Any messages for Mom?"

"Say *Come home SOON.*"

Tilly ran into the school. The bell was ringing.

Everyone in her class was already sitting at their tables, reading. Tilly slipped into her place next to Susila. Mrs. Almond was reading a book too.

"OK," Mrs. Almond said to the class, as usual. "Start bringing yourself back from the story world. Find a good place to leave the story for now." She put her own book down on the desk. "Later on today, we're going to be sharing our *own* work-in-progress and helping each other with editing and revising our stories."

Tilly thought about her story. Did she really want anyone else to hear about her secret fox? The story was in her notebook, deep at the bottom of her bag, still unfinished. But now it was time for math. There was no point worrying.

At recess, Susila asked her about the baby.

Tilly described how tiny he was. "This big," she said, holding out her hands.

"Sweet," Susila said. "I can remember when both my brothers were born. Can I come and see him?"

Tilly felt herself flush. "Yes," she said. "When he's home. You can come and play after school today, if you want."

"Yes please!" Susila said.

And now it was the afternoon, and time to work on their stories. Tilly got hers out of her bag.

"You've written a lot," Susila whispered. "Mine's only short."

"Take turns to read what you've written aloud, then listen to what your partner has to say: the things they like, the questions they have, any suggestions," Mrs. Almond said.

"You go first," Susila said to Tilly.

Tilly took a deep breath. She moved her chair around a little, so no one else could hear. She started to read her story about the fox and the girl.

"You're supposed to say what to do to make it better," Tilly said when she'd finished reading.

"I don't know," Susila said. "I loved it all. Just write some more, and make it have a happy ending. I don't like sad endings for stories."

"I don't know what the ending is," Tilly said. "It hasn't happened yet."

"You mean, it's all for real?"

Tilly nodded.

"Will you show me the foxes if I come to your house?"

"Yes. But don't tell anyone."

"Promise," Susila said. "Cross my heart and hope to die."

"Your turn now," Tilly said.

Susila's story was set in London, about a girl who was an orphan. "It's not about me," she said. "It's all made up."

"The descriptions of the house are good," Tilly said. "You make it sound amazing. The girl living by herself and everything."

"She couldn't do that in real life if she was eleven," Susila said. "But so what?"

Granny was waiting at the school gate.

Tilly and Susila ran over.

"Can Susila come home with me today?"

"Of course. Hello, Susila!" Granny said. "Have you asked your mom? Shall I have a word with her?"

"She's not here. I walk home by myself usually," Susila said. "It's only around the corner."

"Do you want to borrow my phone, then?" Granny got her cell phone out of her bag and handed it over.

Tilly watched Susila chatting on the phone.

Susila nodded and grinned at Tilly. "I can stay till six," she said.

"Good," Granny said. "Tell your mom we'll give you a ride back. Then she won't have to come out to get you."

Granny chatted as she drove them home. She'd been at the hospital before coming to get Tilly. "Your mom sends you a big kiss, and baby sends a little burp."

Susila laughed.

Tilly was quiet, thinking about Mom.

"Your house is huge," Susila said as they climbed out of the car. "And there's a garden and everything! It's like a house in a story."

"It's freezing cold and very impractical," Granny said. "But the garden will be lovely in the summer, won't it, Tilly?"

Having Susila with her meant that Tilly saw everything a bit differently. In her story, she'd made the garden sound bigger and grander. She hoped Susila wouldn't be disappointed when she saw it for real. They walked all the way around, and Tilly showed Susila the flowers hiding under the dead leaves and the way the birds flew down for bread crumbs and the robin almost tame enough to take cheese from her hand, and then she showed her the way out of the metal gate, across the path, to the wild garden behind the flint wall, through the rickety wooden gate.

But here too it all looked smaller and more messy and drab than when she came by herself. There seemed to be fewer trees, even.

"Is this where the fox lives?" Susila asked.

"Yes. In the bramble bushes. Ssshh, now."

They crept closer to the tangle of dead branches and leaves and thorns. It was bitterly cold. The wind carried tiny bits of ice, like frozen rain. There was no sign of the foxes. They waited. Nothing stirred. The brambles looked empty of life.

Susila was shivering.

"We may as well go back," Tilly whispered. "Nothing's going to happen here today. It's too cold." She didn't show Susila her own den. She had the strangest feeling that Helen might be there, and she didn't want her to see Susila. She didn't know why.

Granny had made them tea.

"Let's explore the house!" Susila said. She wanted to look in all the rooms, even Dad's study. She thought everything was amazing. "So many rooms!" She ran along the landing and shouted, so she could hear the way her voice echoed from the high ceilings.

The house had never seemed so alive!

Downstairs, Granny turned up the radio.

Now what? They'd run out of things to do.

"We could go on your computer?" Susila suggested. "What games have you got?"

"None," Tilly said. "I don't even have my own computer."

"What do you usually do, then, when you're at home?"

Tilly thought for a bit. "I read. And I play outside. Sometimes I watch TV or DVDs." She nearly mentioned the dollhouse but that sounded much too babyish. "I know!" Tilly said. "We could go and look in the attic."

Together, they tugged the ladder from the spare room onto the landing and set it up beneath the trapdoor. Tilly went first, to open the hatch, and Susila climbed up close behind.

"Wow!" Susila said. "Look at all this old stuff! It's like an antique shop!"

"There's a chest full of old clothes," Tilly said. "Want to see?"

They pulled out armloads of clothes and started

trying them on. "Careful where you step," Tilly said. "You don't want to go right through the ceiling."

That made Susila giggle—that and the funny clothes. They pranced around in front of an old mirror they found stacked up next to loads of old, framed pictures. The pictures were paintings mostly, and some more photographs, like the ones in Dad's study. There was one of a girl. Tilly pulled it out to look. A girl with dark-ish hair in a woollen dress stared back at Tilly, out of the spotted old photo. It was the same girl who'd been in that other photo before, but older. More like twelve or thirteen.

"Helen," Tilly whispered.

"Who? Who's that?" Susila asked.

Tilly put the photo back down on the floor. "No one, I mean, I don't know," she said.

Susila looked at Tilly. "She's like the girl in your story."

"Yes."

"But this photo is really old. Like, it's from the olden times."

Tilly didn't say anything.

Downstairs, Granny was calling their names. They both stood still to listen. They heard footsteps and then

Granny was calling again, up into the attic. "Tilly? Susila? Whatever are you doing up there? It's time for Susila to go home."

They pulled off the clothes, stuffed them back into the chest, and went back down.

Granny fussed about the ladder. "I'm not sure how safe it is. I wish you'd told me that's what you were doing, Tilly."

"Sorry," Susila said.

"Never mind now. Get your things together and I'll take you home."

The house seemed so quiet now, without Susila. Tilly flopped down on her bed. It had been nice having a friend to play with again. It was a long time since that had happened, what with the move and everything. The time had just whizzed by. She thought about Susila's house when they'd dropped her off: the big family of children crowding around Susila's mom at the door, all the chatter and noise and pushing and shoving and questions. It was a little like Ally's family.

Next time, perhaps she would pluck up courage to show Susila her den. And with any luck they would see the fox cubs together.

And Helen? Tilly didn't know *what* to make of her and the photograph in the attic and the garden that was sometimes there and sometimes not.

Dad sat on Tilly's bed. He was so tired he kept yawning. He nearly fell asleep when he was reading the next chapter of Tilly's bedtime book.

"Dad?" Tilly said. "How can something be there and not there? Is it possible?"

Dad perked up a bit. It was the sort of question he usually loved. "Well," he said slowly, drawing out the word. "At the same time, do you mean? Or sometimes it is there and other, different times, not?"

"That. The second one."

"Hmm. What sort of thing are we talking about here? For instance, something simple, like ice? Ice is sometimes there, on a cold day, and sometimes not, when it's warm and sunny, for example."

"No! Not like that. That's obvious," Tilly said.

"What then?"

"A person. Or a place. That is sometimes there and at other times it isn't. Or you can't find the way in."

"Well, people come and go. But a place, that's a little different. You expect a place to be there all the time. Unless it's a dream place, I suppose, or an imaginary one, like in a story. Is that what you mean?"

"I don't know really," Tilly said.

"That reminds me," Dad said. "Granny says someone's started working on that old garden next door. Clearing it up. Cutting trees. Perhaps someone's bought the place. Maybe we'll get new neighbors. Someone else for you to play with. That will be good, won't it?"

What about Helen? And the foxes?

Tilly felt angry with Dad suddenly, as if it was all his fault. "You can go now," she said. "I want to go to sleep."

"Me too!" Dad stood up, stretched, and yawned again. "Unfortunately, I've got work to do first. I haven't written a word for days. Night night, Tilly. Sleep well."

Don't say it! Tilly thought. *Don't say "sweet dreams."* She pulled the blanket up over her ears so she wouldn't hear.

Chapter 24

The fox padded on velvet paws. Her amber eyes gleamed in the strange light—not normal dark, but the magic half light reflected from new-fallen snow. Snow speckled the red-brown hair on her back. She placed each foot carefully into the cold snow, leaving a line of neat prints across the snowy garden. Every so often she stopped, her black nose twitching, listening out for danger. In her mouth she carried the limp body of a dead mouse, still warm.

The tiny cubs were waiting for her, deep in the den beneath the tangled thorny stems of the blackberry bushes. She had been gone a long time. Hunting was hard in the snow. Most mammals were hiding or hibernating, curled up deep down in their own burrows, and

the mother fox was exhausted—and extra wary; she had spent most of the day listening to strange sounds, loud voices, machines, whirring, and sawing, a horrible whining, screaming sound. Every hair on her body had stood alert. Was the danger coming closer? She would have to make a new den, in a more hidden, secret place away from noise and people. She had already sniffed around an old, disused badgers' sett in the horses' field. That might do; it was dry and quiet, away from people and machines. She would have to move the cubs one by one, carrying them by the scruff of their neck, through the cold night. But first she had to feed them.

Chapter 25

It was snowing again, just like Granny had predicted. Tilly ran silently across the garden, picking her way across the grass and through the damp undergrowth.

Tilly let out a huge sigh of relief. Helen was waiting for her, huddled in their den. She was wrapped up warmly in her old-fashioned green woolen coat with the velvet collar and two rows of brown leather buttons, a long black skirt, lace-up boots.

Helen patted the ground next to her. She put her finger to her lips: "Sshh!"

Tilly wriggled inside the den and sat down.

Helen pulled the blanket over both their laps.

Tilly could see the trail of her own footprints, leading the way from the gate across the garden and another set of tracks, small and neat and closer together. "The fox?" she whispered.

Helen nodded. "Watch," she whispered.

Tilly shivered. She heard something scrambling, and then a flurry of snow blurred her vision, but suddenly right in front of her was the fox, carrying a tiny cub by the scruff of its neck, in her mouth. She plodded through the snow to the gate and disappeared.

"What's she doing? Where's she taking it?"

"She's moving the cubs somewhere else. Something must have frightened her. The garden isn't safe anymore."

It was painful, watching the vixen make her slow journeys with her babies in her mouth. Tilly wished she could help. Where was the male fox? It looked like such hard work, carrying the cubs like that, through the snow, in the dead of night, all by herself.

She made three journeys. They waited for her to come back a fourth time. But nothing happened; there was no sign of her. Just the cold creeping in, and the snow settling deeper. Even huddled under the blanket, close up to Helen, Tilly was freezing.

"Maybe there were only three," Helen said. "That was the last one."

"So tiny!" Tilly said. "Weren't they? Will they survive?"

"I hope so," Helen said. "I expect they are tougher than they look. Like human babies."

"What if she's forgotten one? Or something's happened? Supposing she's left one behind in the old den?"

"She might leave one if it was sick or too weak, the runt of the litter." Helen said very matter-of-fact. "She has to do what's best. There's no point if it's not going to survive."

"Survival of the fittest? It's horrible. I'm going to look. Just to make sure."

Helen pulled her back. "Don't be silly. If the vixen *does* come back and sees you, she'll abandon the cub anyway, because you're there. And if the cub's too tiny and weak, what can you do?"

"I can try and save it."

"How? You can't give it what it needs. You can't keep a fox as a pet. That's cruel."

Tilly remembered a story Mom had read her once, about a girl and a baby piglet who was going to be killed because it was the runt of the litter. The girl, Fern, saved the piglet and looked after it. She fed it milk from a baby's bottle. But that was a piglet, not a wild fox cub.

"I've got to go back now," Helen said. "And this is the last time I can come and see you. I just came to say good-bye, really."

Tilly's eyes filled with tears. "Why?" she said.

"You'll be all right now," Helen said. "You don't need me any longer."

"What do you mean?"

But Helen didn't answer. She hugged Tilly tight for a second. "I'm glad we saw the cubs, even though it was for such a short time. Perhaps you'll see them when they're bigger. They'll come back to the garden to play and hunt, I expect."

Tilly crawled out of the den. "I still don't understand. Why do you have to go? Please explain…Where are you going?"

Helen was already running, fast and light, toward the trees.

Tilly watched her, dazed. She didn't even try to follow. The snow seemed to glow, bright as daytime. She looked up at the sky. The snow was coming down thicker and faster now. Huge, soft feathers, swirling and dancing and spinning down to earth.

When she looked for her again, the girl had vanished. Not a trace remained: her footsteps had already been completely covered up by snow. It was as if she had never even been there in the first place.

Chapter 26

Tilly woke up in her bed. It was early morning, and the room glowed with the strange light reflected off snow.

Snow!

Last night!

Everything flooded back. The fox and the tiny cubs being carried by the vixen, one by one, and Helen...

Saying good-bye.

The last time.

Sadness flooded over her. And at the same time, she remembered something else. Today was the day they'd find out about Mom and the baby and the tests at the hospital.

Granny bustled into the bedroom. "Good morning, Tilly! Have you seen outside? If it carries on like this, there won't be any school today!" She pulled the curtains back. "And more snow is forecasted for later today! Isn't that exciting? It doesn't snow for nearly twenty years, and then it snows twice in one month!"

"Can we go sledding?" Tilly asked. "Can we take Susila too?"

"We'll see," Granny said. "We don't even know about school yet. You'd better get ready just in case."

Dad was already in his study. As she went past on her way down to the kitchen for breakfast, Tilly could hear him tap-tapping his story on the computer. One word and the next, and a sentence and another.

Granny put a bowl of porridge on the table for Tilly. She made herself toast and coffee. "We'll put out food for the birds in a minute," Granny said. "And something tasty for your fox."

Tilly stared at her. "My fox?"

Granny laughed. "All that food disappearing from the fridge! I knew it wasn't you eating it, Tilly!"

"She's got cubs," Tilly said. "And she had to move them because of the trees being chopped down."

"No one will be chopping down trees today," Granny said. "Not in the snow."

The telephone rang. Granny went to answer it.

Tilly's heart beat faster. That might be Mom.

Granny called out for Dad to come to the phone.

Tilly listened, trying to guess what was happening. But Dad was just saying *Umm* and *Yes* and *Of course,* so it was hard to tell. Then it was her turn.

"Tilly?" Dad called her over. "Mom wants to talk to you." He handed her the phone.

Mom sounded just like Mom—like the old Mom, before she got ill. "We're being sent home this weekend!" she said. "Isn't that the best thing ever?"

"What if it's still snowing?" Tilly said. "What if the car can't get to the hospital?"

"I'll walk if necessary!" Mom said. "Nothing's going to stop me. I just want to be home now, with you and Dad. I've had enough of being cooped up here."

"We've got everything ready," Tilly said. "The baby basket and the clothes and everything."

"What else have you been doing?" Mom asked.

"School. Writing a story. I had a friend over to play."

"Wonderful," Mom said. "The baby wants to talk to you. Do you mind?" There was the sound of the phone being fumbled and put down and then picked up again, and then silence.

"Say something, Til." Mom's voice came, a bit distant.

"Hello, Toby," Tilly said. "Or Todd. Or Norbert."

"He's listening. He's blowing bubbles. He's poking out his little tongue!"

"Charming!" Tilly said.

Mom laughed.

Tilly heard a faint squeaky sound and then the beginnings of a hungry-baby cry, working itself up to a full-blown wail.

"Nothing wrong with his lungs," Mom said. "It's feeding time at the zoo; I have to go. But it's not long now until I can see you. Just a few more days. I miss you, Tilly! Love you!"

"I love you too," Tilly said. She put back the phone.

"You're jumping up and down like a—like I don't know what!" Granny said. "I assume it's good news?"

"She's coming home this weekend." Tilly was smiling so much her cheeks began to hurt.

Granny turned the radio on. She pressed the buttons till she found the local radio station. The traffic news came on, and then something about sports, which Tilly ignored, and then a woman started reading out a list of schools closed because of snow.

"Northfield Elementary!" the woman said.

Tilly, Dad, and Granny cheered.

"Give me another hour on my book," Dad said, "and then let the sledding commence!"

"We'll phone Susila," Granny said, "as soon as we've cleared up."

Tilly pulled on her too-tight boots and grabbed her coat and ran out into the garden. The birds flew down from the tree for the toast crumbs. Tilly filled the birdfeeder hanging on the tree with more seeds, and then she waited for the robin to come for his piece of cheese. That done, she ran in big circles around the snowy garden, covering it with a maze of boot prints. She found a perfect, smooth place for making angels; she flopped back onto the snow, swooshed her arms up and down to make the wings, and got up carefully, so as not to spoil the angel shape. She practiced until she made two perfect angels: one for her, one for Helen. Then she did one more for Susila.

She went to the garden gate; there were tiny V-shaped prints of birds, light on the ice crust on the surface

of the snow, up and down
the snow-covered lane, and
other tracks: rabbit feet, she
recognized, and there—
at last, a little to the
right—the   deeper
prints of her fox.

Tilly followed the
neat prints right to
the end of the lane,
as far as the gate to
the horse field, and
then she stopped. The
prints kept going, into the
field, across to one side, and disappeared
over the brow of the hill. The field was empty, a
smooth, beautiful mound of perfect snow, almost blue,
and pink at the edges where the tree shadows fell. No
horses today. There was nothing to stop her from going
on; the tracks would lead her straight to the new den.
It was obvious now. She could find it easy as anything.

But she didn't.

If I follow her now, Tilly thought, and she hears me,

smells me, she won't feel safe. She'll look for another den. Move the babies all over again. It's not fair.

Helen was right. You couldn't really be friends with a fox. That moment, ages ago now, when she'd reached out her hand and touched her fur, and the times she'd held out food and the vixen had taken it, that wasn't fair either. The vixen had been hungry and desperate; that's why she'd come so close. And if by chance she did start trusting Tilly, it wouldn't be good for her, not really. She was a wild animal, not a pet.

Tilly ran back down the lane, back through the gate, across the garden to the kitchen.

"I'll phone Susila," she told Granny.

They had one red plastic sled between the four of them, so they took turns. Then Tilly and Susila squeezed up together in the sled, Susila at the front, to make the long whizzing slide down the hill above the school. They shrieked and giggled as the sled bounced and careened off at an angle and dumped them in a heap at the bottom of the slope.

"We never did this in London. We never even had snow," Susila said, laughing. "I never had so much fun. Ever!"

"We've never had it before either," Tilly said. "Not deep like this."

They picked themselves up and trudged back up the hill for the next go. Tilly's face tingled with cold. Her boots were full of snow and her mittens sopping wet, but she was happy. She hadn't laughed so much in ages. When Granny took her turn on the sled and it went sideways and shot into the hedge and Granny had to bail out and landed in a heap of wet snow, Tilly thought she'd be sick she was laughing so much.

Granny laughed till tears rolled down her cheeks.

"Back for lunch?" Dad said eventually.

Dad heated up soup while Granny went for a long, hot soak in the bath.

"I'm soaked through!" Susila said. "Can I borrow some dry clothes?"

Tilly and Susila trooped upstairs together. They slid along the shiny edges of the hallway in their damp socks.

Tilly opened the wardrobe for Susila to choose some clothes. She picked out blue jeans and a black sweater, and sat on the carpet in Tilly's bedroom to pull on a pair of pink fluffy socks.

"What's that?" Susila said, pointing. "Under your bed?"

Tilly flushed. "It's my old dollhouse," she said. "I don't play with it anymore."

"Why not? It looks amazing! It's really old, isn't it? Like that other stuff in your attic. Can I see?"

Tilly helped her slide it out from under the bed. They blew the dust off the top of the tiled roof.

Susila lay on her tummy so she could look through the windows.

"It's got lights and everything!" she said. "But no furniture."

"I put it all away," Tilly said. "But I know where it is. I can get it if you like."

"Yes please!" Susila said.

Tilly rummaged in the wardrobe again. The box was hidden under a pile of old sweaters. She opened it up to show Susila.

"Little pictures and pots and pans and beds and everything! Let's put it all in the house."

Tilly opened the front up. "It's all a little dusty," she said.

"Wow! Wallpaper! With roses on!" Susila said. "That's like in that story you wrote, about the girl. She had rose wallpaper." She picked up the table and the chairs and arranged them in the kitchen. She put the beds upstairs. She found the tiny cradle at the bottom of the box. "This is so sweet! You should get a tiny baby doll to go in here! Like your real baby. When's he coming home?"

"Saturday." Tilly's face felt hot.

But Susila didn't notice anything. She was too busy, getting the furniture out, rearranging things, putting the dollhouse people together into the kitchen, around the table, playing happy families.

And now Dad was calling them down for lunch.

Susila had gone home. Dad was working in the study: "My last chance," he said, "before Mom gets here tomorrow with the baby, and all our lives change forever."

Tilly lay on her bed to think about what would be different.

Mom would be up and about. Granny would go home. Mom would have the baby to look after, but babies sleep lots, especially to begin with, Dad said. So Mom would have time to spend with Tilly again. And when the baby grew a bit bigger, Tilly could help look after him. She could play with him, show him things. She could read books to him and tell him stories and make him laugh. And at school, now, there was Susila to be friends with.

Tilly pulled out her notebook from under her pillow and leafed through the pages of her story.

Make it have a happy ending, Susila had said.

She picked up her pen and turned over a fresh page and began to write.

Outside, the sun came out, briefly—a pale wintry February sun, like a promise of spring.

Chapter 27

Tilly woke up very early. The first birds were singing their hearts out, and it was beginning to get light. The room was full of gray, soft shadows; the familiar shapes of her bookshelves and the toy chest, the wardrobe and her table and chair and the dollhouse all looked slightly different, like ghosts of their real selves.

Tilly's heart was beating fast, like it did when something amazing was about to happen. She crawled out of bed and pulled back the curtains to look out.

The pearly light transformed the garden too. The grass was silver; the tree a dark presence, its arms stretched out against the sky. The flowers under the tree were pale yellow stars.

Something moved through the gray bushes near the gate. Tilly watched.

The fox stepped onto the lawn, head down, tail level with her back. She sniffed and stopped and waited. She looked up at the window, right at Tilly, and Tilly looked back.

I'm coming! Tilly mouthed silently.

She got dressed quickly, pulling on jeans and a T-shirt and a thick sweater and socks, and then she opened the bedroom door very quietly, and tiptoed along the landing, past Mom and Dad's room. The door was ajar; she glimpsed their sleeping shapes close together under the blanket. On the floor next to the bed was the baby's basket and the white mound of blanket and one tiny hand, poking out, next to his small head with its funny fluff of dark hair. Today was the day baby Toby should really have been born. A kind of extra birthday, Tilly thought.

Tilly crept downstairs into the kitchen and pulled on her new waterproof boots—a good-bye present from Granny. She turned the key in the lock and opened the back door and went out. She walked as quietly as she could, stepping on the damp grass, leaving silver footprints.

The light was already stronger; the sun was coming up, and the garden was alive with birdsong. It was like stepping into another world—a place which belonged to birds and wild things, not to people, Tilly thought—all busy with its own life. She was a visitor there.

The fox had gone, but it was easy enough to follow the silver prints of its feet over the grass, through the gate, turning right up the grassy path to the field.

She stopped at the stile. The horses were back; one stood motionless, one foot slightly raised on the edge of its hoof, as if it had been frozen like that, a statue, except that its warm breath made clouds around its muzzle, and the air fizzled and steamed like a halo. Every hair on its back was lit up by the early morning sun.

She heard the fox bark, and then, like a reply, high squeaks and whimpering sounds. She held her breath.

Ohhh! At last! There they were: first, the vixen, followed by one, two, three small furry cubs, bounding and tumbling at the edge of the field. She watched the cubs play like puppies, until finally the vixen trotted on and they rushed away after her, toward the trees and out of view.

Tilly smiled. How amazing was that?

She waited, but they didn't appear again. Her hands and face were freezing. She turned away from the field and walked back along the path. She hesitated a moment at the rickety gate and then slipped into the wild garden, even though it belonged to someone else now. They hadn't repaired the wall or the gate yet; she didn't think they'd mind.

The sun warmed her back. She crossed the grass; under last year's dry, dead, old grass, new shoots of green were beginning to sprout. Beneath the lavender hedge, snowdrops were already in bloom, as were papery thin white flowers like a delicate, smaller kind of daffodil. Small pale red leaves were unfurling at the end of the twigs on the old rambling rose. The wild garden was springing into life.

She went to have a look in the old den. It smelled of damp earth inside. Part of the roof had collapsed. Next time, Tilly thought, I'll make a tree house, high up with the birds, with air and light all around. Me and Susila can make one in the apple tree at the end of our garden.

Something caught her eye. What was it? It looked at first like a small dead creature with matted fur, half-buried in the dead leaves. Tilly crouched down to look properly.

After all this time! Little Fox, tattered and moth-eaten and frayed at the edges, looked back at her. She picked him up, brushed off the dirt, smoothed him down, and kissed his threadbare head. "Welcome back!" she whispered.

Tilly traced her steps back to her own garden. She began to notice all the things changing here too. Flowers pushing up through the dark soil, like Granny had talked about. The tree next to the shed was covered in small white buds, ready to burst into blossom. She knelt down to pick one of the yellow star flowers under the big tree: eight fine yellow petals and a green-gray leaf in the shape of a small, perfect heart.

Mom was in the kitchen, waiting for the kettle to boil. She looked up, startled, as Tilly came in the back door.

"Whatever…?" Then she smiled. "You're an early bird!" she said. "I thought I was the only person in the whole world awake so early! What have you been doing, Tilly?"

Tilly placed the little yellow flower on the table and put her arms around Mom. Mom's pink dressing gown was soft and warm against her cold face.

"A celandine!" Mom said, looking at the little flower. She kissed Tilly's head. "So pretty! So full of hope!"

Tilly squeezed Mom tight. "I saw three baby fox cubs, for real, in the field at the end of the path," she said. "And look who else I found!"

She opened out her hand to show Little Fox's face peeping out.

"Your funny old toy fox! He looks as if he's had a few too many adventures!" Mom said. "He needs a good wash and mending. He's getting very old! But I'm glad he's come home at last."

"Yes," Tilly said. "Everyone's home now."

Mom poured tea into her best blue cup.

Tilly frothed up the warm milk for her with Dad's whisk, and she poured the rest of the milk into her own favorite pink mug with roses. She settled down next to Mom at the table.

Nestled up close with Mom, in the sunlit kitchen, Tilly felt the warmth begin to tingle back into her cold fingers and toes.

On the wooden table, the celandine flower glowed, a small golden sun.

Author photograph © Kim Green

JULIA GREEN is the author of more than ten novels for children and teenagers. As a child, Julia lived in a village called Ashtead, in Surrey. She received a degree in English at the University of Kent and an MPhil in English Studies at Oxford University. Julia lives in Bath and is Course Director for the MA in Writing for Young People at Bath Spa University. She has two sons. You can find out more about Julia by going to her website at www.julia-green.co.uk